Painted Devil

Painted Devil

MICHAEL BEDARD

Atheneum 1994 New York
Maxwell Macmillan International
New York Oxford Singapore Sydney

Atheneum
Macmillan Publishing Company
866 Third Avenue
New York, NY 10022

Macmillan Publishing company is part of the Maxwell Communication
Group of Companies.

Published simultaneously in Canada by Lester Publishing Ltd.

First edition

Printed in the United States of America

10 9 8 7 6 5 4 3 2 1

The text is set in Electra.
Book design by Claire Naylon Vaccaro

Library of Congress Cataloging-in-Publication Data
Bedard, Michael, [date]
Painted devil / by Michael Bedard. —1st ed.
p. cm.
Summary: A visit from strange Aunt Emily invokes in Alice a foreboding
sense of evil, as they find connections between the local library's collection
of old puppets and a sinister magic show that took place twenty-eight years
earlier.
ISBN: 978-1-4169-6139-0
[1. Puppets—Fiction. 2. Fantasy.] I. Title.
PZ7.B381798Pai   1994
[Fic]—dc20   92–35637

For Isaac and Kirsten

ACKNOWLEDGMENTS

I would like to express my thanks to the staff of Boys and Girls House of Toronto, and in particular to Joanne Schott, for making their extensive collection on puppetry available to me in researching this book. Thanks also to the staff of the Moose Jaw Public Library for kindly providing me with archival material on the history of the library.

On my volcano grows the grass
A meditative spot—
An acre for a Bird to choose
Would be the General thought—

How red the Fire rocks below—
How insecure the sod—
Did I disclose
Would populate with awe my solitude.

                    —Emily Dickinson

Painted Devil

Part One

Ladies and gentlemen, how do you do?
If you are happy, I'm happy, too.
Stop and hear my little play.
If I make you laugh, I need not make you pay.

—Punch's Prologue

1

DINNER WAS DIRT, A GENEROUS PLATE-
ful for each, with a side dish of straw-colored grass
freshly pulled from the lawn, and a teacupful of
sand to wash it down. The dolls were no doubt hungry after
the long months they had spent in the shed, sleeping quietly
in their rusty carriage while winter covered them in forgetfulness.

Lela set the table for them in the sandbox, shaking out
the dusty flannel sheet they had been swaddled in, spreading
it carefully over the damp sand, ferreting out the set of plastic dishes kept with the dolls in the carriage. She set four
places, one at each corner of the sandbox, and sat the dolls
down.

Alice sat nearby, observing the ritual. Her little sister was
turning her clothes into a muddy shadow of their former
selves, but she was happy at least, and the house would be
quiet while her mother slept.

She sat as stiffly in her chair as the dolls at their dinner,
afraid to move, afraid that so much as breathing too deeply
would send the rickety thing collapsing in a heap to the
ground. It too had been rescued from the shed, the only
chair still in one piece that she'd been able to find in there,
an old wooden recliner with a slack canvas seat. As if resent-
ful at having been shut away so long, it dug its legs deeply
into the sodden lawn.

Spring had taken Alice completely by surprise. Suddenly
there was sun, warm sun, and flowers doggedly blooming
amid the litter of dead leaves that lay like a dingy blanket

over their beds. Had she been feeling ambitious she would have fetched a rake from the shed and begun to work some of the dead stuff away.

Ambitious, however, she was not. The sun was too wonderfully warm on her face. She felt it seeping into her, burning off the long lethargy of winter, filling her with that heady sense of newness that comes with spring.

Beyond the sandbox and shed, past the weathered wooden fence at the foot of the yard, lay the woods. Part of the strip of railway land that ran through town, they were the last remnant of wilderness in the midst of civilization.

As she sat staring into their green shadows, she thought of Mother lying in the shadows of the upstairs room, her belly big with the new life that harbored there. And yet again she relived that day two weeks before when she had hurried home through the woods.

She'd been coming back from the library and had taken the shortcut over the tracks and through the trees, full of news of her day. The bare limbs had just begun to leaf out again, and the woods were suddenly alive with the scurrying of unseen creatures in the undergrowth.

She had found the house strangely silent when she came in, silent with the strangeness of things not being right. She moved through the kitchen slowly, like one caught in a dream. In the doorway she stopped short.

Mother was lying motionless on the living room couch, chalk white, a towel tucked between her legs.

"Mom, what's wrong?" She was never sure whether she actually voiced the question or simply felt it thundering through her, but her mother opened her eyes, took her in as she stood paralyzed in the doorway, and smiled weakly.

"It's all right, dear. I've had a bit of bleeding. I called your father. He should be here any minute now." Already the weak attempt at a smile had disappeared, and a chill silence had fallen over her face.

Alice didn't know what to do, what to say. Mother looked like a statue of spun glass as she lay there. She wanted to run and take her mother in her arms, but she feared that if she touched her, she would shatter into countless pieces.

Alice unfolded the blanket lying across the foot of the couch and covered her. Again that weak, remote smile, the useless reassurance that everything would be all right.

It seemed hours before Father arrived, the smell of sawdust still strong on him from the butcher shop where he worked, a spot of blood on his sleeve. He took one look at Mother lying there and hurried her to the hospital.

She had stayed there for two days, undergoing a battery of tests. They found that there had been a slight abruption of the placenta, the baby's life-support system in the womb. She returned under strict orders that she rest, remain in bed as much as possible. Another such incident, they warned, would put the pregnancy at risk.

Since then Mother had spent much of her time confined to the shadowed room at the head of the stairs. Mrs. Morrison, a neighbor down the street, came in to watch Lela during the day for them. Still, a hush lay over the house now, the sense of things holding their breath. A sudden fragility had entered into their lives.

The dolls made a strange sight, sitting there in all degrees of undress and disarray, with wide startled eyes, not yet used to the sudden light, still dreaming doll dreams in their stuffed or hollow heads. Lela moved among them, ministering to each, urging spoonfuls of mud and grass against their unmoving mouths, chattering cheerfully all the while of what treats lay in store for them if they ate their dinner up.

The outside dolls were a sorry-looking lot, and looked sorrier by the minute as dirt clogged their puckered lips and rained down their fronts. There were the Raggedy Ann and Andy dolls that Alice had played with as a child. Both of them were all but bald now, their bright woolen hair reduced to a few sad tufts about the ears; the stitched-on features of their faces had come unraveled; so that Andy's eyes were all but absent, and Ann's mouth was little more than two turned-up corners with nothing in between. It made it difficult for her to eat her dinner.

Beside them sat the rubber doll with the scribbled face. She had always been a sad-looking thing, even when she'd lived indoors with the other dolls, a poor relic passed down to them by Mother. A deep cut ran across her forehead and the eye below it no longer closed. The stiff stubble of her shorn hair stood straight up from her head as if she were in a more or less permanent state of shock. None of the doll clothes ever quite fit over her unyielding arms and legs, with the result that even in the dead of winter she went naked.

Last spring Lela, almost four, had decided to cheer the poor dear up a bit by decorating her face with colored markers as she sat drawing at the kitchen table one day. It was doubtful whether the green and red streaks that now graced her forehead and cheeks had really cheered her up. Certainly she looked as forlorn as ever, shivering miserably in her corner of the sandbox as Lela tried to coax sand through the small bottle hole in her mouth.

"Lela, stop that," said Alice, as calmly as she could manage. The least hint of tension and the chair would have its revenge. The two of them, she suspected, were in league. "You're going to get her all full of sand."

"But she's hungry."

"Then just pretend you're giving it to her, okay?"

"This isn't pretend," said Lela. She gave Alice the indignant glare of an outraged mother.

"Lela, stop it or I'm going to get up out of this chair and take you back inside."

Lela gave her a long look, as if she might just be willing to test the seriousness of that threat. The spoon hovered uncertainly in the air for a moment, then showered sand down harmlessly into the box.

She moved on to the last of her charges, a large stuffed doll that Mother's sister had sent them from Victoria two Christmases ago.

The doll had always seemed out of place, dominating the other dolls that lived in the house; Lela had quickly lost patience with its stitched-on clothes and had abandoned it to the yard. After spending the winter doubled up in the doll carriage in the dark of the shed, it was probably wishing it was back in Victoria about now.

Lela gave the doll a sidelong look as it sat slumped in its corner of the sandbox staring vacantly off into the woods, then dutifully offered it a drink of dirt. But there was no love in it, and when the doll refused, Lela flung it unceremoniously out of the sandbox onto the wet grass and hurled its plateful of grass and sand after it.

The game was over. The sad remains of the dinner were dumped on the lawn, and Lela had begun to bury the dishes in the sand. It was definitely time to take her in.

Alice eased herself out of the chair—which promptly collapsed onto the grass. She picked it up, returned it to its rusty nail on the inside wall of the shed, and gathered up the dolls, folding the large doll into the carriage first, then settling the others around it, along with the sandy dishes. She wheeled the whole sorry lot back into the shed and was all but ready to shut the door on them when she caught sight of the naked rubber doll peering imploringly over the edge of the carriage at her.

For some mad reason, she simply didn't have the heart to shut it away again in the dark with the other lost dolls. She plucked the poor thing up, then shut the door and returned the rusty lock to the hasp.

Lela had already run off ahead of her; she was sitting on the porch steps, shaking sand from her shoes. The lid of the sandbox was leaning against the back fence. Alice sat the doll down on the edge of the sandbox and went to get it. Her eyes settled again on the woods.

The damp smell of leaf mold and growing things rolling off them would normally have intoxicated her, but now she found it strangely unsettling. It seemed as though they lay under enchantment, like the magic woods in one of Lela's fairy tales.

Settling the lid over the sandbox, Alice scooped up the doll and hurried toward the house. Lela gave her a disapproving glance when she saw the doll.

"She's an outside doll," she said. "Mama said she's an outside doll."

"I think she'd like to come in for a little while, Lela. She says it's cold in the shed without her clothes, and she doesn't like the dark."

Lela looked skeptically at the doll, its shock of stubble hair, its scribbled face.

"She didn't really say that," she said. "That's just pretend."

Nonetheless, she took the doll from Alice and disappeared with it through the door.

Alice stood alone for a minute on the porch, knocking the last of the sand from Lela's shoes, looking out over the woods.

"No, Lela," she said to herself with a certainty that shocked her. "This isn't pretend."

2

PARKVIEW PUBLIC LIBRARY WAS A queer old building, one of those faded testaments to an earlier time, which the age had somehow overlooked and therefore spared. In spirit it was classical, with its stately columns and rounded arches. But there was that of the Gothic where the stonemason had left his mark. Carved birds formed the brackets below the eaves. The tops of the twin pillars flanking the entranceway were adorned with dragons swallowing their tails. And from the cornice they supported, a gargoyle peered out through a pattern of leaves.

Years of city soot and weathering had marred the finely tooled work. And there was something unsettling in those silent figures now, something that caused the younger children to glance up uncertainly at them as they mounted the stairs, and to scurry quickly past.

Inside, time had been kinder. The dark stained-oak furnishings and woodwork had aged with a quiet gentleness that recalled a simpler time. And the mazes of high, closely placed bookcases wound off to alcoves and secluded corners where one could readily lose oneself in dreams.

It was mainly children who used the library now. Others had forgotten it. Graduating to the corner-store paperback stand and the television set, they had consigned it to the quiet oblivion of childhood. There were of course those few old patrons, remnants themselves of another age, who returned religiously each week with their bundle buggies and stooped backs to ferret through the dusty shelves for biographies and murder mysteries. But in the main it was to children that the place had fallen.

The late Miss Witherspoon, who had been librarian there for forty years and whom only death had managed to coax from behind the counter, had never quite come to terms with this change and was always wondering why there were so many ruffians underfoot. She had allowed the juvenile collection to atrophy at some point about thirty years past, when children had ceased to conform to the rigid picture she possessed of them.

Yet up until her death, she still continued to devote considerable time and energy to a long-standing tradition at Parkview—the Saturday Morning Club, an old-fashioned weekly session of storytelling and puppet shows over which she presided.

Near the end, both she and it were looked on with quiet amusement as relics of the past. But in her prime, Miss Witherspoon was said to have been a marvel, particularly in the production of puppet shows. Some of the older patrons who had seen these early shows as children spoke with something approaching awe of her amazing skill, of the painstaking care that went into the puppets she made, and above all, of the aura of magic that accompanied those shows.

All that was history now. The only thing that remained of it was the ornate wooden puppet theater pushed up against the wall in a remote corner of the Children's Room, its paint dull and chipped, its faded velvet curtains permanently closed.

The abandoned puppet theater was but one sign of a more general neglect that clung not only to the forgotten corners of the library itself but extended as well to the land on which it sat.

The library had been named the Parkview with a purpose. When its doors had first opened many years ago, to much fanfare in the local papers, the press of the day had heaped praise not only on the structure itself, with its marble rotunda and stained-glass dome, but also on the park in which it stood.

The following from the *Caledon Daily Examiner*, August 10, 1918, is typical:

> The handsome new Parkview Public Library was formally opened last Saturday evening in a ceremony attended by local dignitaries and presided over by Mayor Davis. Crowds thronged the handsome building and the picturesque park in which it is situated.
>
> A more ideal setting can hardly be imagined than is occupied by this fine public library, surrounded by lush flower beds and overlooking the pleasantly wooded banks of the Rouge River. . . .

The flower beds were still there, though "lush" would hardly be the appropriate description of them now. Each spring the city would send out a crew to turn up the soil. They would dutifully set out the standard show of begonias and impatiens in an alternating pattern of spokes radiating from a hub of roses, water it faithfully over the next couple of weeks, then quietly leave it to the mercy of the weather and the weeds.

By late June the summer heat would have withered the impatiens, the begonias would have dropped their blooms, and the denuded rosebushes would be left in thorny solitude surrounded by their dead.

Once a month a stray worker would suddenly materialize and make slow circles around the property on a tractor mower, cutting down the crop of dandelions that sprang from the scorched grass, setting out the sprinklers to fan apathetically back and forth for the afternoon and tempt the grass to green.

The limit of his care extended only so far as the six-foot chain link fence that ran across the rear of the library property, separating it from the wild strip of railway land and the woods beyond.

There were still faint traces of an old flagstone path that had launched off from a now-abandoned reflecting pool behind the library. It dipped beneath the fence and was quickly lost in the long grass. In former days, one walking this path would have been led on a pleasant stroll into the shade of the woods and ultimately down to the banks of the Rouge River, where wrought-iron benches were ranged beneath the trees for one's repose.

The Rouge was a cesspool now, thanks to years of raw sewage and factory effluent being belched into its once pure waters. It had died a slow death while the city cast a blind eye in its direction and busied itself with the more rewarding allures of concrete and steel. As the office towers downtown had quietly multiplied like mushrooms in the dark, the older neighborhoods near the river had been allowed to languish, unwelcome reminders that even skyscrapers cast shadows.

With the decline of the river, the neglect of the woods soon followed. Fewer and fewer souls strolled the paths through them, with the result that those paths became progressively narrower and at last the wilderness reclaimed them as its own.

With the wilderness came the rumors—rumors of danger in the woods, the specters of rape and robbery raising their ugly heads. Up went the fence to ward them off.

It was a rare sight now to see someone entering the woods, save for the occasional band of children seeking adventure, or the inhabitants of the houses on the far side of the river taking a shortcut to the bus stop by the library or to the few stores along Parkview that still had not closed their doors.

Mr. Dwyer, the new librarian at Parkview Public, was a tall, intense creature with an inherent nervousness about him that had somehow settled in his hands, long thin hands that were never still, it seemed. It was those hands that Alice first noticed about him when he appeared one day behind the desk recently vacated by the late Miss Witherspoon. As they fluttered down on the stack of books she had just returned, Alice was reminded of large white butterflies touching tentatively down on flowers.

Over the course of the years he had managed to encase the rest of his body in the cool chrysalis of the professional. His hair was short and thin, his glasses round, his clothes deliberately dull, dignified in a slightly rumpled sort of way, his voice pitched just a touch lower than it really wanted to go. He had studied long, one sensed, in aging himself beyond his years, in winding himself completely in that consciously aloof cocoon.

Somehow the hands had escaped. Refusing to be ruled, they had fluttered free. They were the hands of a child— curious, restless hands like Lela's, incapable of lighting on any one thing for long; timid, easily startled hands, the hands of the small boy hidden inside the shell. She found she could not stop looking at them.

He grew aware of her watching as he busied himself with the books, carefully removing the cards and setting them to one side, tallying the inevitable fines on a sheet of scrap paper plucked from a wooden box on the counter. Parkview Public did things the way they had always been done.

"Fairy tales," he said suddenly, as if to distract her from his hands at their restless work.

"Pardon?"

"You seem to like fairy tales," he said, fixing her with wide, intense eyes.

"Oh—they were for my little sister. She loves fairy tales. Just gobbles them up."

"Ah," he said, "so do I." And he smiled a little smile that she instantly realized had escaped as well. He flipped through the books, reading off the titles.

"*Bluebeard, Beauty and the Beast, The Seven Ravens.* Ah, *Jorinda and Joringel,* now there's a frightening story for you: the magic wood, the witch turning all those children into birds and shutting them in cages in her castle. How old is your sister?"

"Nearly five."

"And she's not frightened by some of this stuff?"

"You'd have to know my sister. She likes to be frightened—as long as it's not right before bed."

"I guess we're all pretty much the same," he said, and laughed. "Something inside us craves that thrill of fear, especially when you can close the covers on it afterward and tuck it safely away on the shelf."

He pulled the cards from the pocket of the last book on the pile. Her library card was among them. He glanced at it and paused momentarily before he passed it to her.

"Alice. Alice Higginson. Now why does that name seem to ring a bell? We haven't met before, have we?"

"No, I don't think so."

The hand fluttered down the column of figures on the scrap paper, tallying the fines owed.

"Let's see now. That comes to a grand total of forty-seven cents."

15

As she rounded up the stray change in her pocket, he continued repeating her name over to himself, trying to figure out where he knew it from. She was four cents short.

"Don't worry about it," he said. "What you've got there will do just fine."

She dropped the pennies in his palm, the hand closed slowly over them, and at just that moment he gave a little cry of success.

"I've got it. I know where I've seen your name before. Did you apply for a job here a while ago?"

"Yes, that's right." She'd almost forgotten. It had been more than a year and a half ago now when, in a pinch for funds, she'd filled out an application under Miss Witherspoon's wilting eye. "Too young" had been the official pronouncement at the time, but they'd keep her on file.

"Isn't that strange," he said. "I was just going through the files this week, as a matter of fact, rooting out some of the deadwood. You wouldn't still be interested in the job, would you? I really could use a student assistant. There's an awful lot of work that needs to be done around here—as you can no doubt see. The pay isn't great, but the work is interesting. And there's this little project I—"

He stopped in midsentence, embarrassed by his own excitement. His hand fluttered up to his face, settled briefly on the frames of his glasses, then flitted down to the counter. He pinioned it under the other to keep it there.

"Think about it," he said with a shy smile.

Think about it she did as she roamed the old wooden stacks looking for something for herself, finding nothing, then settling finally in the little nook in the Children's Room where the picture books were shelved. Another fix of fairy tales for Lela. As the pile grew beside her on the floor, she glanced around the room: the old puppet theater against the wall nearby, the big bay window looking out on the woods behind the library, the old-fashioned wooden furniture. It would be kind of nice working here, quiet, peaceful. She could use a little of that. Besides, there was something intriguing about this new librarian, something in his shyness that she liked.

As she was leaving that day she told him that she was interested. A little more than a week later she started working at Parkview Public, two afternoons a week after school and all day Saturday.

She had been there for less than a month when she hurried home through the woods that afternoon and found Mother lying on the living room couch.

3

ALICE SAW LELA STATIONED AT the front window as she turned up the walk to the house. She watched her put her mouth close to the glass, mist it with her breath, then slowly shape the letters of her name. When she caught sight of Alice coming up the porch stairs she smiled and waved excitedly, then ran to open the door.

Alice stood patiently on the porch, listening to her sister struggle with the lock, watching the mist fade from the window. The lilac bush against the house had burst into bloom and the air was heady with its scent.

"Guess what?" cried Lela when she had finally succeeded in opening the door.

"What?"

"Mama's come down. Come see."

Mama had indeed come down. Lela practically dragged Alice into the kitchen; and there she was, large as life, sitting at the table and chopping celery for the salad while Mrs. Morrison worked at the sink.

It was strange to see her downstairs, suddenly among them again. Over the past few weeks she had faded to something of a ghost, a figure swaddled in bed sheets, tucked away in an upper room, emerging periodically to waddle down the hall to the bathroom and back. It was shocking now to see her in the brightly lit kitchen, the bulge of her belly resting so solidly on her lap; it was as if they had dreamed the whole thing.

"Surprised?" asked Mother, smiling up at her. She had

tried to chase the paleness from her face with lipstick and a touch of rouge, but shadows still clung to her eyes and the back of her hair bore the impress of the pillow. She turned to take a kiss on the cheek.

"Shocked would be a better word. Are you sure you should be down here?"

"Yes. It's fine, really. The doctor just said to take it easy. He didn't say I couldn't get up."

Mrs. Morrison looked over from the sink and shook her head. "Mr. Higginson will have my head for this," she yelled. You could have heard her clean out to the curb. Mrs. Morrison shouted everything she said; her husband was hard of hearing and years of living with him had ruined her for quiet conversation. Half an hour with her and you found yourself hoarse from hollering back.

"Just you leave Mr. Higginson to me," yelled Mother. "Honestly, I couldn't stand it up there alone another minute. I felt like I was melting away. You might have come up with the supper tray tonight and found nothing but a little puddle on the bed. I'm finished with the celery, Mrs. Morrison. Maybe we should chop up a couple of tomatoes." She went to stand.

Mrs. Morrison swung around from the sink. "Don't you dare budge from that chair," she said. "I'll get them."

Mrs. Morrison was not one to be argued with. She dried her hands briskly on her apron and went to fetch two small tomatoes from the windowsill where they had been set to ripen. She rinsed them at the sink and brought them, still dripping, to the table.

Lela, meanwhile, had wheedled her way under Mother's arm and latched on to her like a leech. She would have crawled up onto her lap, had there been one to crawl up onto. Instead, she contented herself with clutching Mother around the waist, resting her head against the huge belly, listening intently for baby sounds, while Mother patiently tried to work around her.

Father arrived home shortly after six. Mrs. Morrison had made a hurried exit minutes before. He almost had a fit when he saw Mother downstairs; he scolded her soundly, reminded her again of the dire consequences the doctors had warned them of if she failed to follow orders.

Mother sat quietly weathering the storm, chopping a green pepper into tiny and tinier pieces. When she was done, she scraped them into the salad bowl, kissed him on the cheek, and told him to go wash for dinner. He obeyed her like a little boy.

Now as she took Lela upstairs to get her ready for bed, Alice listened to the faint murmur of conversation from the living room, where Father sat with Mother on the couch. She had put up a brave front, but by the end of the meal all the rouge and lipstick in the world would not have been able to mask the fatigue on her face. There was a brittleness about her now that could not be simply wished away.

Several of the stairs creaked. It was an old house, one in a series of squat row houses erected more than a century before. Who knew how many people had walked these stairs since then, each bearing his own burden. The stairs creaked now under this new one as Alice followed Lela up into the shadows of the upper floor.

Downstairs the ceilings were high, and though the rooms were small, they breathed, as Mother would say. Upstairs they did not so much breathe as gasp for air. Now, as the night drew near, it was as though the weight of darkness had buckled the walls, bringing the ceiling down so low that you could feel it hovering ominously overhead.

They tiptoed past the room at the head of the stairs, its

door closed, the pale light of a lamp seeping beneath it to wash the worn linoleum of the hall; past the dim room, once Alice's, that was now to be the baby's. The small white crib sat empty in the shadows, a mobile hung motionless above it, its bright baubles suspended in the air like planets frozen in the night sky. The room itself seemed frozen now, as though all that lay within its whitened walls had turned to ice.

Lela cast a wary glance within as she hurried by.

Their own room, at the far end of the hall, was the largest of the bedrooms. It was also the one least touched by time. There was an odd air of forgetfulness about the room, as if it were not quite convinced that time had indeed passed since those first feet had ascended the stairs.

It sat there now in its antique wallpaper dress as they came in and switched on the light, like an old woman whose mind moved in small slow circles, and whose visitors, whoever they might be, would always wear the faces of those same few dear ones, now long dead.

The window shuddered lightly in recognition as Alice quietly closed the door. Lela ran to the bookcase by the bunk bed they shared and began rooting furiously through its contents for her favorite, an old book of myths and fairy tales that had been in the family since Mother was a child. The signature on the flyleaf of the book was her aunt's— Emily Endicott. Above it was another, stroked-out but still readable: "Irma Potts 1931. Grandma gave it to me."

Somehow it had survived the years, though not unscathed. Its binding was cracked, and the board covers clung by a few stubborn threads to the spine.

A *Wonder Book of Tales for Boys and Girls*, proclaimed the ornate black lettering on the front. Lela could point out the words *book* and *boys and girls*, but *wonder* was quite

21

beyond her, and *tales* made her laugh, for she somehow imagined they would open the book and hundreds of tails for boys and girls would rain down on their laps.

She found the book and ran over with it tucked under her arm to choose the fortunate doll that would sit with them in the corner to share the story today.

The inside dolls were a select few. Amanda, the most recent among them, was an Italian doll with a stuffed cloth body and rubber head and limbs. She slept in a cradle by the bed in her pale blue nightgown, dreaming of far-off places, and could not be disturbed. Sarah, the brown-skinned doll, slept beside her. Over by the window, Jessica and Jasmine, a pair of rag dolls with black button eyes and stitched-on smiles, shared tea at the little table. Jasmine, a boy doll fated to wear dresses and bear a girl's name, sat stiffly in his chair and stared miserably down at his pink pinafore. He had hardly touched his tea.

Lela hovered over them an instant, debating which to choose. Then her eye fell on the sad doll with the scribbled face; she lay alone by the toy box, staring up at the ceiling through an eye that would not shut. She was wrapped in a flannel blanket, for the clothes in the doll drawer would not fit.

Lela snatched her up and carried her over to the corner. She handed Alice the book, and sat down on her lap with a thump.

"I want the one with the wolf," she announced.

"You mean 'Little Red Riding Hood'?" Alice looked at her doubtfully.

"Yes."

"But I thought your dolls were scared of that story."

"They are, but not this one. This one likes to be scared."

Alice glanced down at the stiff scraggly hair, the wide

dark eyes, and the permanently puckered lips of the doll. She had certainly had her share of shocks, not the least of which must have been being locked away in the shed last winter.

"What's her name?" she asked.

"Asha," said Lela instantly.

"Asha? That's a strange name. Where did you get it from? Did you make it up?"

"No," said Lela defiantly. "She told me it was her name."

The trouble with living with Lela was that after a while you got so that you more than half believed her when she came out with something incredible like this.

She had breathed a sort of life into these cloth and rubber creatures, so that now even when you were alone in the room you were never really alone; for they were there with you, lying stiffly in their beds or staring fixedly in front of them, as if they were looking through things into some strange, unchanging world of their own.

Since moving back in with Lela, Alice had become completely infected by it. It had reached the point, in fact, where she could not stand to see one of them lying facedown on the floor but would have to pick it up and put it right. And more than once she had found herself kneeling by the nightlight in the dark, dressing some doll that had been left naked in the cold, before she could climb up to her own bed with a clear conscience and sleep.

Life had been so much saner before, when the small room next door had been hers. At least then there had been some refuge. Now there was none. She had been just on the brink of finding some pattern to her life, of seeing things assume some final order, when suddenly she had been hurled back into chaos.

How incredibly bitter she had been when Mother and

Father broke the news of the pregnancy to her and at the same time told her of the plan to move her in with Lela. It was purely a temporary thing, they assured her—at most a year or two—and then the room would be hers again. They might as well have said an eternity.

On the eve of the move, she had lain awake in the lost room, lain awake for hours, with the walls bare and her life in boxes around her, and sensed that she was being shipped back into childhood.

And it was then, out of sheer frustration and despair, that she had done it, wished the dreadful wish, which some primitive part of her feared lay behind all that had followed: the wish that the baby had never been.

All this passed swiftly through her mind like the pages flipping past as she thumbed through the book, searching for "Red Riding Hood." It was somewhere near the back, in the section of the book devoted to fairy tales, past "The Tinder Box" and "Bluebeard" and "Hansel and Gretel." Lela hovered over the pages like a cat about to pounce, one plump hand poised in the air. It was the pictures that she loved. They positively terrified her, but they could not pick up the book without Lela poring over each one they passed with a dread fascination.

The hand came down now, in "Hansel and Gretel," at the picture of the witch peering out the window.

It was a truly unsettling picture, imbued with a quiet, creeping horror that even Alice was not totally immune to. Today, the picture would never have appeared in a book for children. There was too much of the dark about it. It was as if the unnamed artist had touched his pen to the nerve of terror at the very heart of the story.

At first sight it seemed innocent enough. Hansel and Gretel stood wide-eyed before the little house in the clearing. The bricks of the house were loaves of bread; the roof was shingled in sugar cakes; icing hung from the eaves. Gretel had just broken a piece of bread from the wall. Hansel had snapped a bit of icing off and was about to eat.

Yet all about them one sensed the sinister presence of the woods through which they had been wandering for days. They encroached upon the clearing on all sides, throwing long creeper-laden limbs onto the room of the cottage, watching with dull wooden eyes that had opened in the trunks of the trees.

Suddenly one's eye was drawn to the window. And what at first had seemed like the shadow of an overhanging limb on the glass became, on second sight, a skeletal arm draped in rags, resting against the inner frame of the window. And from under it peered a horribly thin face so withered that it looked as if it had been fashioned from the fissured bark of trees—as though the wood itself had taken human shape.

Alice felt Lela's body tense on her lap as the child studied the witch staring out the window at the children as hungrily as they looked at the house. Lela hunched her shoulders and sucked the breath between her teeth.

"She's a bad witch," she said, clutching the doll close.

"Yes," said Alice. "Very bad."

"She wants to eat Hansel and Gretel."

Alice nodded, shifting the small hand from the page, fanning quickly to the story near the back.

"If I was there I'd chop her all to pieces and put her in the fire," said Lela emphatically.

Footsteps on the stairs: Father bringing Mother back to her room; the quiet creak of the door opening down the hall.

She found the page. "Little Red Riding Hood," she read, guiding Lela's finger along under the ornamented lettering of the title.

"Once upon a time there was a little girl, dearly loved by all, especially by her grandmother. She had made a red cape for her with a hood, like the ones fine ladies wear when they go riding. And it suited the child so that soon everyone called her Red Riding Hood. . . ."

Alice felt Lela slowly relax into the story, lulled by the rhythm of the words. The doll on Lela's lap listened too, and the two at the table, and perhaps the two in the cradle also listened in their sleep. The room itself seemed to shift slightly in its wallpaper dress and strain to hear.

Shadows of voices drifted down the hall. The words rolled off her tongue effortlessly, as if the story told itself. The window shuddered lightly as the night leaned its velvet arm against the glass and looked in.

4

THE MACHINE HAD JUST EATEN another library card, the third one that day. Five people stood waiting in line, their arms laden with books, while Alice switched the stupid thing off and on, off and on, trying to coax it to cough up the card. It was like trying to get Lela to give up a mouthful of candy.

The off-on technique had worked with the other two, but this time the machine was having no part of it. It sat there humming contentedly to itself while it quietly consumed the card. The old woman the card belonged to stood at the counter with a worried look on her face, her head shaking gently from side to side. The longer it took, the more it shook. A couple more minutes and it would fall right off onto the floor.

Alice smiled weakly up at her.

"It's being a little temperamental today," she explained, switching the machine off and on again, this time giving it a little shake.

Had she been home, she would have given the blasted thing a good bash over the head. But this was the library; one must be calm, cool, collected at all times. The closing buzzer sounded again. Someone in line coughed peevishly into her armload of paperback romances. Alice ran to fetch Mr. Dwyer.

She found him in his office, a room still dominated by the imposing portrait of Miss Witherspoon, who stared down from the wall above the desk with a reproving glance at the changes that this intruder had dared to make to her domain. Decades of quiet disorder, which had been allowed to creep unchecked to every corner of the room, had been cut away. The desk now was clear of clutter, the books on the shelves were free of dust. The boxes of ancient rubber stamps and antiquated book cards, relics of a system no longer in use, had been relegated to the garbage bin. Miss Witherspoon did not appear at all pleased.

Mr. Dwyer was bundling together yet another box to be put out at the curb after closing, when Alice came in. He glanced up and smiled.

"All done?"

"No, not quite—the machine's acting up again. There's a card jammed in it and I can't get it out. A bunch of people are waiting in line."

"Oh, wonderful."

They returned to the counter together. The natives were growing noticeably restless, breathing audibly down their noses, glancing fretfully up at the clock. They had places to go, people to see, things to do. Standing in line in a semidarkened library on a Saturday night was not their idea of fun. The old woman's head was wobbling like a loose wheel.

Mr. Dwyer took a letter opener from the drawer, turned the machine on its side, and began poking tentatively around the rollers inside, cursing quietly under his breath. He turned it back on. The gears seized up again as the machine clung stubbornly to the card, like a dog to a meaty bone. Mr. Dwyer stood back, took one long icy look at it, then smacked it hard with his hand.

The machine gave a startled little yelp and instantly spat the card out onto the counter. It was hopelessly crumpled and riddled with greasy teeth marks from the gears of the machine. The old woman looked on with alarm while Mr. Dwyer calmly smoothed it out, smiled, and handed it to her. She was still trying to fit the twisted thing back into the plastic window of her wallet when he finished charging out her books.

Five minutes later the last of the patrons were out the door. Mr. Dwyer threw the bolt and drew the blinds. The building settled into stillness around them. Pale motes of colored light danced on the floor beneath the stained-glass dome set high in the ceiling above.

In the dimness, time dissolved. Shabby and down-at-heel in the daylight, the building resurrected itself in the dark. The past, so carefully labeled and shelved, awoke, arose. It might have been 1918 again.

Here, truly, was a place out of time. The two of them suddenly seemed pitifully small and insignificant standing there. Beneath a flimsy shroud of dust, something stirred. As she stood within its spell, Alice had the sudden unsettling feeling that anything might happen here.

"Care for a coffee before you go?" asked Mr. Dwyer, startling her. "There's something I'd like to talk with you about." He led the way past the desk and down the narrow hall beside the office into a small workroom at the back of the building. This was the room where new books coming into the library were processed and old ones repaired. The shelves were lined with stacks of both. Spools of colored cloth tape for mending damaged spines, pots of glue, and boxes of book pockets and blank catalog cards littered the scarred wooden worktable in the center of the room. An old manual typewriter teetered on the edge of the table, as if it might be contemplating suicide.

The sleek new coffeemaker on the counter looked decidedly out of place, an interloper from another era. The dark aroma of coffee filled the room, masking the dusty smell of books. Mr. Dwyer took down two coffee cups from the shelf above the counter and filled them.

"Black okay?"

"Fine," she lied.

He brought the cups over and pulled a couple of chairs up to the table. They settled in front of the steaming coffee. Out the back window she saw the high electrical tower stationed just beyond the library fence, holding its skein of wires aloft in the still air. Past it lay the rusted track and then the woods. If she could see through the woods, there would be her house.

Mr. Dwyer fiddled absently with an empty ashtray on the table. His hands, though considerably less agitated now than they had been when Alice first met him, still had a life of their own.

"You can smoke," she said.

"Ah, you read me too well." He reached for the package in his pocket. "Am I really that transparent?"

"Not really." She watched him shake out a cigarette, light it, and toss the spent match into the ashtray. He looked around him.

"This room is definitely the next item on the agenda," he said. "You know, it might sound funny, but I can't shake the feeling that our dear Miss Witherspoon has not quite departed her post here. I keep having the unnerving sensation that she's standing just behind me.

"She was like a spider in a barn; she spun to her heart's content here for years, totally undisturbed. Now, suddenly, someone is mucking about in her business, undoing all of her work. I keep walking into webs wherever I go. And I can't help but feel that sooner or later I'm bound to bump into the spider herself. Forgive me—that's a terrible thing to say. She was probably a very sweet old lady."

"Maybe. But she kept it well hidden. She used to scare the life out of me."

"Well, I can't say I'm surprised. If that picture is any indication, she was a pretty formidable woman." The hands were quiet now, momentarily distracted by the cigarette, like a fidgety child by a toy.

"How's your mother doing?" he asked.

"Oh, better. She's up and around a little more now. She was bored to death just lying in bed all day."

"How much longer does she have to go?"

"About two months—the middle of August. But the doctor says she'll likely deliver early."

Mr. Dwyer leaned back in the chair, running his hand through his hair. She noticed the tiny hole in his left earlobe. He had worn an earring once, perhaps still did in other circumstances, in the part of his life lived beyond the walls of the library. He was handsome in a quiet sort of way, though most people probably wouldn't think to look at him twice.

"All right. I'll come clean," he said. "Remember that special project I mentioned when we first met?"

"Yes. You never did say exactly what it was."

"No, I wanted time to think about it. I guess I wanted time to see whether you'd settle in here, too. Well, unless I'm terribly mistaken, you do seem to have settled in. So I've been thinking about it a little more again lately." He butted the barely smoked cigarette and leaned forward across the table. "Did you ever see one of the puppet shows Miss Witherspoon used to put on?"

Instantly the image of the abandoned puppet theater sitting in the shadows of the Children's Room leaped into Alice's mind.

"Oh, yes. I used to come every Saturday when I was small."

She remembered the old woman sitting in front of the puppet theater, reading from a storybook while she waited for the crowd to gather. With her shrill old voice, and her knobbly fingers holding open the pages of the book, she had reminded Alice then of the witch in the *Wonder Book*.

"I understand she was very skilled," he said.

"Yes, very." She had been old enough by then to know that the puppets had no life of their own, that it was the old woman who gave them movement and voice. But she was so incredibly good that you forgot she was there at all. There was not a hint of her voice to be heard in the puppets' voices, not a trace of her anywhere, except perhaps when there was a frightening figure in the show. Then the shrill voice took the stage, and sometimes Alice swore she could see a papery face peering through the backdrop at her. Even now the memory sent a shiver running through her.

"She wrote a book on puppetry, you know," said Mr. Dwyer. "It's still highly regarded in the field. I found a copy among her things in the office." He pointed to a thick book in a chipped dust jacket lying on the table between them. *The History of the Glove Puppet*, she read on the spine.

"I read it for the first time back in library school," he went on. "It was probably that book more than anything else that sparked my own interest in puppets."

"Oh, I didn't know you were interested in puppets."

"Yes, very much so. It's sort of a secret passion, you might say. That was why I jumped at the idea of coming to Parkview when I heard there was an opening. I knew about the collection that was housed here."

"Collection?"

"Yes, a very fine collection of puppets. You see, Miss

32

Witherspoon not only made puppets for her shows, she also collected them. Because of her expertise in the field, she did a good deal of traveling, and in the course of her travels she collected a large number of rare and valuable puppets. For all I know, she may even have used those puppets in the performances she gave here at the library.

"When she died, she specified in her will that the puppet collection was to be left to the library, with the provision that it continue to be housed and maintained here. One of the reasons I got this job was because of my experience with puppets; part of my job is to see to the collection.

"Which brings me back to the project. You see, I thought it might be a good idea to start up the Saturday Morning Club again. It needn't be every week. Once or twice a month would be more than enough to begin with. And I was rather hoping you might be interested in helping me out. You know, cleaning up the puppet theater, deciding on a play, working the puppets with me backstage.

"But perhaps it's too much for you to take on now. With your mother not well, I'm sure you have your hands full as it is. In any case, why don't you think about it over the weekend, talk it over with your folks, and let me know what you've decided next time you come in. All right?"

"All right."

"Well, it's getting on. I'd better get you home before they begin worrying about you. Why don't you take that copy of Miss Witherspoon's book along with you? You might find it interesting." He collected the cups, dumped the dregs down the drain, then made a quick pass through the building while Alice gathered up her things and waited by the main desk.

She could hear the whisper of footsteps in the dark, the eerie whistling on the floor above. From where she stood she could see into the Children's Room. The wide bay window framed a view of the woods. The sun hung above them, a ball of flame. Her eye fell on the puppet theater half hidden in the shadows of the room. For a moment she imagined someone was standing behind the closed curtain, peering silently through the crack.

5

PUNCH AND JUDY

I

*Curtain opens on scene 1—*PUNCH's *house, a view of a garden.* PUNCH *is heard behind the scenes, singing. He appears.*

PUNCH: Judy. Judy, my sweet. Where are you, my darling? (*to audience*) You haven't seen her, have you? Well, you must meet her. (*knocking on playboard*) Judy, my dear.

JUDY (*below*): What do you want?

PUNCH: Come here, my dear. (*aside*) Isn't she a sweet thing? The voice of an angel.

JUDY: I said, what do you want?

PUNCH: Come upstairs, my sweet. I want to speak to you. Ah, here she comes now.

Enter JUDY.

JUDY: Well, here I am. What do you want, now I've come?

PUNCH (*aside*): Isn't she a beauty? Now, there's a nose for you.

JUDY: What do you want, I say? I've things to do; the dinner's on.

PUNCH: Ah, don't be cross, my dear. Give us a little kiss. Just a little one (*kisses her; she slaps him on the face*). Oh, what a smack that was.

35

JUDY: There. How do you like my kisses? Will you have another?

PUNCH: No, no, my dear. One is quite enough. (*aside*) Always joking, my Judy is. Where's the baby, my sweet? Bring me the baby, Judy. And mind you don't drop the dear thing.

Exit JUDY.

PUNCH: Ah, there's a wife for you. Isn't she a wonder? And such a beautiful baby. Wait till you see. Such a sweet disposition—just like his daddy. Ah, here's the darling now.

Reenter JUDY *with the* BABY.

JUDY: Here, you mind him while I finish the dinner (*hands him the child*).

PUNCH: Ah, come to Daddy, dumpling.

JUDY: How awkward you are.

PUNCH: Nonsense, I can mind him just as well as you can. Just leave him with me.

Exit JUDY.

PUNCH (*singing as he rocks the baby in his arms*):

> *Hush-a-by, baby,*
> *On the treetop.*
> *When the wind blows,*
> *The cradle will rock.*
> *When—*

(BABY *cries*)

PUNCH: Ah, what's the matter? Poor thing. It has a stomachache, I dare say. Be still, my sweet (*bumps the baby up and down*).

> Hush-a-by, baby,
> Sleep while you can.
> If you live till you're older,
> You'll grow up a man.

BABY (*cries*): Mam-ma-a-a!

PUNCH (*taking the baby and rolling it back and forth on the stage*): Judy—Judy, my love. I know what's the matter. He's hungry, that's it. I'll get him his milk. Don't cry, my plum—here's your bottle.

(BABY *hits it out of his hand, and cries louder still.* PUNCH *picks up the baby and bangs its head against the stage.*)

PUNCH: Now, be quiet, will you? Be quiet. Ah, such a beautiful child. He has his father's nose. (BABY *grabs him by the nose.*) Eee! Eek! Murder! Let go. Oh, my nose, my beautiful nose. There, you little devil, go to your mother if you can't be good (*throws* BABY *out the window*).

6

THERE WAS A BATTERED OLD CAR, pocked with rust, parked in front of the house when Mr. Dwyer dropped Alice off. It hadn't seen the inside of a car wash in a long while. The grime on the windows was so thick she could barely see inside. From what she could manage to see, though, the backseat was a chaos of clothes, books, and cardboard boxes. It looked as if someone had settled in to live.

"Hey," she called as she came through the door, "did you see that old rattrap out front? I wonder where that crawled in from?"

It was then she noticed the bulging old suitcase, held closed by a leather belt, standing at the foot of the stairs. A limp cloth coat lay draped over the newel post above it like a ghost hovering over an unquiet grave.

"Mom? Mrs. Morrison?"

"In the kitchen," called an unfamiliar voice.

As she crossed the living room and came warily into the kitchen doorway, Alice saw Lela perched on the lap of a woman she'd never seen before.

Her hair was reddish, parted in the middle and drawn back into a band on one side. The other side hung loose and full down past her shoulders. A pile of bobby pins lay on the table in front of her. She was reading Lela a book, altering the story at will as she went along. Lela kept glancing up at her to make sure they were reading the same story. The woman wet a finger, flipped the page, and reached up to snare another pin. Her eyes fell on Alice, standing dumb-struck in the doorway.

"You don't know me," she said as she drew the loose hair back off her shoulder and began to pin it in place. Only her earlobes, pierced with pearl studs, showed below the auburn sweep of hair. "I'm Emily—your mother's sister." She let her large dark eyes linger an instant before flitting back to the book.

Aunt Emily! The picture of the doll doubled up in the shed flashed through Alice's mind—memories of cryptic, all-but-illegible letters postmarked from all parts of the country, birthday greetings arriving apparently at random through the year. Mother had always said her older sister was a little odd. Here was living proof.

"And the gingerbread boy ran on faster than before. But the fox ran close behind, and he would have caught that lit-tle gingerbread boy and eaten him all up, if they hadn't sud-denly come upon a big old car parked by the side of the road. And that old car swung open its door and said, 'Hop in, little gingerbread boy, we're heading the same way, you and I.'"

Lela looked down at the picture, then up at her, then back at the picture.

"It doesn't say that," she said.

"Sure it does, right there." Aunt Emily ran her finger under the mythical words. There was a mischievous twinkle in her eye.

"So the little gingerbread boy hopped into that big old car and they drove off down the road, leaving that bad old fox standing there watching till they were gone. The end."

She closed the book and set Lela down on the floor.

"So much for rattraps," she said with a shy smile as she

slid the last pin into place. She looked like something out of an old book.

Lela was sitting on the floor at her feet. She had opened the book again and was busy looking for the elusive picture of the car by the side of the road.

"I'd better freshen myself up a little before your father gets home. He's likely to have a heart attack if he walks in and finds me here like this."

She scooped up the remaining pins and dropped them in the pocket of her sweater. Her clothes were strictly rummage sale: the shapeless sweater, the long pleated skirt, the scuffed black shoes. Definitely an outside doll.

"I put together a little tray for your mother," she said, noticing Alice's gaze. "She's resting in her room. Why don't you take it up to her?"

The tray was sitting on the counter: a glass of juice, a plate of crackers and cream cheese, with a little mound of green stuff that looked like grass on top of each one. It looked like something Lela might feed her dolls. Alice picked it up and started for the stairs.

Mother was sitting up in bed reading when Alice came in. The window was open and a stiff breeze was blowing the curtains around. Alice set the tray down on the bed.

Mother took one look at the green stuff on the crackers. "Emily?" she asked.

Alice nodded. "Where on earth did she come from?"

"I'm not quite sure. The last I heard she was visiting your uncle Albert on the West Coast. Would you mind closing the window, dear? Emily thought I might like a little fresh air. I think I'm catching pneumonia." She picked up one of the crackers, studying the green stuff closely. "I think it's alfalfa sprouts. I've seen them at the grocery. Probably very good for you." She nibbled tentatively at a corner.

"Not bad, actually." She massaged her swollen belly with her free hand as she ate the cracker.

"How's the Bump today?" asked Alice. It was Lela who'd christened the baby "the Bump."

"Fine. Moving a lot. It seems to have taken a fancy to doing high dives off my rib cage, the little devil."

It was good to see the humor creeping back into her conversation. The past few weeks had seen precious little of that.

"So tell me about Aunt Emily. What's she doing here?"

"There's not much to tell, really. I was taking my nap this afternoon, and when I woke up, there she was, large as life, standing over me. I got a letter from her a few weeks back while she was with Albert, saying that she'd been thinking about us a lot lately, asking if everything was all right. She's always been that way—psychic or whatever you want to call it. I wrote back, told her about the trouble we'd run into with the pregnancy, and that was the last I heard.

"Well, it seems she took it into her head to come and visit us. She said she'd been planning on coming back to Caledon for a while anyway. She's really very sweet, you know. A little strange, mind you—but very sweet."

"That's an awfully long way to come from for a visit. Where's she planning on staying?"

There was a long pause. "Um—would you believe here?"

"You're kidding."

She wasn't kidding. "We really could use her help, you know. It's been a strain on both you and your father over these past few weeks, and I'm not sure how much longer Mrs. Morrison will be willing to watch Lela for us. She's been talking louder than usual lately. Besides, I'm sure Emily doesn't have much money."

"But where will we put her?"

41

"I'm not sure. There's the baby's room." She plucked another cracker from the plate.

"Does Dad know?"

"Well, he knows she's here. I thought it might be a good idea to save the rest till after supper."

Father arrived at a little after eight. Saturdays were busy at the butcher shop and he looked hungry and drained. As usual, he was carrying half a dozen packages wrapped in pink butcher paper and tied with string, along with a pound of butter and a carton of eggs—fringe benefits of the job. There were spots of blood on his white shirt where the apron hadn't covered it.

Lela was already in her pajamas. The suitcase had been tucked out of sight in the closet. Aunt Emily had powdered her face and put a touch of rouge on her cheeks. She looked like a little girl who had gotten into her mother's makeup.

"Emily—how nice to see you." He gave her a quick peck on the cheek, dodging the rouge. "It's been awhile. You haven't changed a bit."

"You lie beautifully, Harold."

"I see you're still driving the same car."

"Oh, I wouldn't dream of trading the poor dear in. They'd only throw her on a heap somewhere. I couldn't stand to do that after all the years we've been together. No, I'll just keep on driving her till she dies in my arms."

Lela gave her another of her looks.

Aunt Emily picked up the packages of meat with barely concealed disgust and tucked them away in the freezer.

"You'd better go wash up," she said. "Dinner's almost ready."

Now, Father was a meat-and-potatoes man from way back. Dinner just wasn't dinner if there wasn't a piece of meat somewhere on the plate. So when he came down with Mother and discovered a yellowish slab lying next to a pile of peas on his plate, his face fell.

"Chickpea casserole," explained Aunt Emily. She sliced another piece and put it on Lela's plate. "Just happened to find a can of them up in the cupboard."

Father was not exactly a model of subtlety; he stared down at the thing on his plate as if it might move.

"What's in it?" asked Mother as offhandedly as she could manage as she passed her plate.

"Oh, lots of good things. Onions, carrots, spices; chickpeas, of course, a bit of white sauce—oh, and a slice of bread to round out the protein. I had to use white. You seem to have run out of brown."

Mother smiled; she obviously didn't have the heart to tell her they never bought brown.

Lela, usually a demon for her food, just sat there with her fork poised over the plate and stared. She had moved her peas as far away as possible to escape contamination.

Actually, it wasn't too bad once you got over the color, and the texture, and the taste of it. Alice managed to choke most of it down, while Mother coaxed Aunt Emily into conversation. She talked about Albert and his family, and Mother's twin, Charles, who taught at a small school in the Midwest. It seemed Aunt Emily spent her time traveling from place to place around the country, supporting herself by working odd jobs wherever she happened to be. She'd picked up the recipe at a restaurant she'd worked in for a while on the West Coast.

There was an odd tension to her talk. She was like a clockwork figure, wound too tight. She spoke swiftly, breathlessly, with barely a glance up from her plate. And when she did look up it was as often as not with a strange fixed smile on her face. One sensed that with years of living alone she had grown unsuited to the company of others.

After dinner, Father and Mother disappeared upstairs, while Alice and Aunt Emily did the dishes. Lela sat at the table with a sandwich. There were a few muffled outbursts overhead, like thunder rumbling in the distance, which they pretended not to hear.

Shortly afterward Father and Mother returned. Father, curiously subdued, settled himself in front of the television to watch the ball game. He might as well have taped a Do Not Disturb sign to his forehead.

The TV was well on its way to becoming an antique. A black band had begun to creep up ominously from the bottom of the screen, stunting the black-and-white figures, warping the flickering world in which they lived. If the set broke, there was no way anyone would have the ancient parts to set it right.

Lela went the rounds giving good-night kisses, planting one squarely in the center of Aunt Emily's rouge. Alice whisked her off upstairs, washed her red lips, read her a quick story, and tucked her into bed.

By the time she got back down, Aunt Emily had settled herself with Mother on the couch. From somewhere she had produced a large embroidered bag of knitting. The rhythmic clatter of her needles punctuated the play-by-play of the TV commentators over the next hour. A pink bootee materialized between the busy needles.

"For the baby," she explained as she lay the tiny thing on the sofa beside her and started casting on the wool for its mate.

Eventually the game wound down and Mother began to make bedtime noises. Father took a couple of trips out to the car with Aunt Emily and carried in a sleeping bag and a few other necessities so that she could bed down in the baby's room for the night. A more permanent arrangement would await the morning.

Alice lay in her bed, waiting for sleep to come. In the bunk below, Lela softly snored. Aunt Emily moved furtively around in the room next door. She must have been pacing, for the floorboards creaked in a repeating pattern.

By the pale glow of the night-light Alice could make out another pattern, that of the ancient wallpaper on the wall by the bed. It was likely the original paper, put up when the house was first built. Mother hated it with a passion and swore that just as soon as the renovations made it up the stairs, it would go.

The paper was done in shades of green, paler in the foreground, but receding by degrees into a dark ground. The pattern was a curious one: a series of vertical bands that looked like nothing so much as bars, but which resolved themselves on second glance into stalks—thick, fleshy stalks with large single leaves launching off from them on alternate sides along their length—and at intervals a branch, on which perched a bird.

The bird was highly stylized—as was the pattern as a whole— and was turned so that its sleek rounded head faced backward. It peered out at the viewer with a wide black eye.

There was something vaguely disturbing about this bird, the same bird repeated endlessly throughout the pattern— something about the glazed, indifferent glance it offered to the world, while its other eye busied itself, one sensed, with something in the darkness behind the pattern.

Some months back, when Lela had been troubled by nightmares on an almost nightly basis for several harrowing weeks, one recurrent dream involved the birds on the wall. She would wake up screaming, flailing at the air, convinced that they had flown down from their perches and were trying to peck out her eyes.

Their beaks were indeed very pointed and the talons, which hooked around the branches on which they perched, were similarly sharp. But it was not the birds themselves that gave Alice occasional pause so much as the suspicion that something lurked in back of the bars of the pattern, something that the birds already saw, but that was as yet invisible to the viewer.

The last sound she heard before she dropped off to sleep was the faint creak of floorboards in the room next door.

The slender figure stood framed in the window of the darkened room, looking out into the night. Balled in her hand was a crumpled tissue streaked with rouge. In the distance, skyscrapers stood defiant in the dark, their silhouettes shredding the horizon, symbols of pride and power.

Here, though, in their shadows grew these woods. She stood watching them now, remembering the many times she had walked through them as a girl, remembering too the ravine into which they had once fed, and the boarded building brooding over it. A faint ripple ran down her spine.

She lit the candle and reached for her notebook. She fanned through to the last entry, written nearly a week ago. A few hurried lines scratched down in the car. Perhaps the beginnings of a poem. She muttered the words below her breath, slowly, deliberately, like an incantation meant to ward off evil.

The candle flared, then guttered briefly as the wax yielded to the flame. The baby's crib cast shadow bars across the ceiling; the mobile hung motionless in the dark. She uncapped her pen and began to write.

She wrote far into the night, setting the fragile wall of words between herself and fear. The candle had burned down to a stub before she finally blew it out.

Sleep brought with it the dream, the same dream it delivered every night now: the dream of a magic show she had attended one August night twenty-eight years before.

7

THE LAST OF THE PATRONS HAD been shooed out early, and the library put quietly to bed. It slept above them now as Alice and Mr. Dwyer went down the cellar stairs.

The ceiling above their heads was made of thick prism glass as old as the building itself. It had been installed as the floor of the archives room and the rare book room adjacent to it to render them absolutely fireproof. A long crack cut through one of the panels—a brief seam of light from the room above.

"They say that happened sometime in the first year the building opened," said Mr. Dwyer, following Alice's gaze. "I'm sure it's perfectly safe."

He walked directly beneath it as if to prove the point. Crossing to a small worktable set against the wall opposite the stairs, he reached up and snapped on a ceiling light.

The shadows, which had until then held sway, scurried beyond the brittle glow of light, slinking behind boxes of discarded books and damaged equipment, shelves of overstock and outdated material, and watched the two intruders with a wary eye.

"Well, here it is," said Mr. Dwyer, running a finger through the dust. "Such as it is." He picked up a small papier-mâché head and turned it in his hand. "This is where Miss Witherspoon worked on her puppets."

The table was cluttered with dusty bits of cloth and felt, bottles of dried paint, pots of glue, and a variety of other odds and ends.

The place had a strange feel about it. Save for the evidence of dust, there was an overwhelming sense that someone busily working here had just been called urgently away, and might momentarily return.

In the middle of the table a large wooden box sat upon a loose bed of brown paper. Severed ends of string hung over the edge of the table. A pair of scissors, furred with dust, lay nearby.

The lid of the box was slightly askew. As she looked at it Alice suddenly stiffened. For an instant, through the narrow crack, she felt sure she had caught the glint of an eye staring at her. When she looked again it was gone.

"This is the collection I've been telling you about," said Mr. Dwyer, running his hand along the ordered rows of cardboard boxes on the shelves beside the worktable. "There must be close to a hundred puppet sets here, many of them made by Miss Witherspoon herself, here at this table over the years. The rest are those she collected during the course of her travels."

Alice scanned the uniform rows of labeled boxes. Familiar fairy-tale titles leaped out at every turn—*Hansel and Gretel, Red Riding Hood, The Frog Prince, Rapunzel*—along with vague memories of shows she had seen as a child.

From the top row Mr. Dwyer pulled down the box labeled *Red Riding Hood* and set it down on the edge of the table. He slid off the lid. Neatly arranged in the bottom of the box, beneath a carefully folded backdrop with a forest scene painted on it, were a script of the show, a number of properties relating to it, and four beautifully worked puppets: Little Red Riding Hood, her mother, her grandmother, and the woodsman.

"Strange," said Mr. Dwyer, rooting through the box. "The wolf is missing. Ah well, it must be here somewhere, I suppose. It likely got put into another box by mistake. Anyway, this will give you some idea of the quality of her work." He had picked up the puppet of the grandmother and was admiring it against the light.

"Just look at the features of the face, the devotion to detail. The wire frame glasses are actually hinged. And see the care that went into the costume. It's all been hand stitched. The woman was truly an artist."

He put the puppet back in its box with something of the same loving care that Lela lavished on Amanda when she was tucking her into bed for the night. Settling the lid back in place, he returned the box to the shelf.

"A puppeteer's paradise," he said, spreading his arms to take in the collection before him. "Of course, the whole place is badly in need of a cleanup. And I'll have to make a complete catalog of all the puppet sets here for the main branch. Miss Witherspoon was not one for keeping records, it seems. I've scoured the office and I can't find a trace of a file. She must have carried all the information around in her head. I don't believe she dreamed she would ever actually die. Maybe none of us really do."

His hands again took on their separate, fretful lives. He let them fuss freely with the things on the table. They tidied some odds and ends, removed the loose paper from under the box, balled it up and threw it in the wastebasket beside the table.

"Alice, I can't tell you how glad I am that you've agreed to help get the Saturday Morning Club going again. I'm very excited by the idea. I've been wondering which show we should do first. There are plenty to choose from, as you can see. But strangely enough"—and here he paused as his hand came down lightly on the lid of the wooden box—"I think it would be fitting in more ways than one to begin with this.

"It appears to be the most recent addition to the collection. It must have arrived just shortly before Miss Witherspoon died. I found a letter on her desk from a dealer in New England named Renshaw. It seems he acquired the set at an estate auction and thought she might be interested in it. It had apparently been tucked away in an attic for years. It's an extremely rare set—truly a remarkable find."

He opened the box. The lid was hinged with wire and brought with it some of the packing straw that filled the interior.

Protruding from the center of the straw, like a body rising from its grave, was the head of a puppet. Its face was the jaundiced white of old ivory; two squat black horns thrust from its forehead; its lean red lips were curled into a terrifying grin.

Instinctively, Alice took a step back from the table.

Mr. Dwyer reached in, carelessly pushed it aside, and felt around in the straw. He came out with quite a different puppet, this one a comical-looking creature with a puckish face and a long, beaked nose that nearly touched an equally long and pointed chin. The figure was dressed in what reminded Alice of a court jester's costume: a loose, belled cap and pied clothes of silk. A large hump protruded from its back.

"This is Punch," said Mr. Dwyer, sliding the puppet onto his hand, brushing off the bits of straw that clung to the costume.

The puppet instantly came to life, looked Alice up and down with an appraising eye, then made a low formal bow. It was obvious at once that here, hidden within the body of the puppet, Mr. Dwyer's hands were for once truly at home.

"Mr. Punch, this is Alice. Perhaps the two of you have met before."

Alice shook her head, and the puppet his.

"Well, I suppose I'm not really too surprised. Punch shows have fallen out of favor these days. A little too crude for today's tastes, I'm afraid, too rough around the edges; perhaps a little too violent for parents' notions now of what a puppet show should be.

"That wasn't always the case, certainly. A couple of hundred years back there were countless Punchmen wandering the streets of cities like London and New York with their portable stages on their backs, setting up shows on street corners and in public parks, attracting large, noisy crowds to watch Punch perform his antics.

"And it wasn't just a children's show then—not at all. People of all ages, from all walks of life, would gather around to watch. In the end, though, Punch always remained the champion of the oppressed.

"But all things pass, I suppose. And eventually Punch landed in the drawing rooms of the rich. He was scrubbed and polished and prettified, and the life was washed right out of him. With the result that now, even in England, his true home, a real Punch-and-Judy show is a rare sight indeed."

He slid the puppet from his hand and settled it back into the box. Again he sifted through the straw. This time he came out with another puppet, a woman in a white bonnet with a small wooden baby in her hands.

"This is Punch's dear wife, Judy. And that's the baby—both of them looking a little the worse for wear, I'm afraid. This is a very old set. According to the letter from the dealer, it is believed to have belonged to Jacob Hubbard, one of the most famous North American Punchmen. He performed in towns and cities all through the East. I believe Miss Witherspoon mentions in her book that he may even have passed through Caledon at one time. When he died the set disappeared; it was believed to be lost forever."

Again he reached into the box. More puppets appeared: a doctor, a policeman, a hangman named Jack Ketch; then, finally, the puppet with the leering white face.

"Horrid-looking thing, isn't it?" He ran his hand across the cracked, rayed paint. "This is the Devil. He appears at the end of the play to fetch Punch away for his wickedness. This is a very old puppet. Much older than the rest of the set, as you can probably tell."

He slid his hand inside the limp black cloth. A tremor ran through the puppet, as if it had been suddenly roused from sleep. It slowly raised its head and looked at Alice. She felt it fix her with its wicked red eyes, and a chill ran through her. It bobbed its head in silent greeting, and the leering smile seemed to widen a little, as though the lifeless wood in fact were flesh. The image of the witch in the *Wonder Book* flashed through her mind.

Mr. Dwyer took the puppet from his hand and laid it back in its bed of straw. He dug down further in the box and came out with a tattered sheaf of papers.

"And this is the text of the play as performed by Jacob Hubbard. This alone, without the set, would be an invaluable find. Next to no records exist of the early Punch-and-Judy performances. Punchmen traditionally passed on the play orally, each making variations on the basic structure of the story as suited him in the actual performance of the play. As a result, it is very hard now to say what an actual performance of the play was like. For some reason, though, Jacob Hubbard or someone close to him decided to write down his play.

"Now here's my idea. In a very real way, the Punch-and-

Judy show lies at the roots of hand puppet shows as they exist today. So why not start up the Saturday Morning Club again with a Punch play? It would be like beginning at the beginning. And to lead off with the last set Miss Witherspoon acquired for the collection would be a fitting tribute to her. I was thinking you could play the part of Punch and I could handle the other characters. Well, what do you say?"

What could she say? His enthusiasm was overwhelming. She smiled and nodded, then watched as he drew the lid of the box closed and secured it with a twist of wire.

He was clearly oblivious of her unease. She was simply being foolish, she told herself. It had something to do, no doubt, with an imagination fueled by too many of Lela's fairy tales; something to do with the shadows massed beyond the tiny island of light in which they stood; with the way the ordered rows of puppet boxes reminded her suddenly of tiny coffins stacked in a dusty vault.

He tucked the box among them on the shelf and gathered up the yellowed script of the play as though it were gold. He turned to her with a smile.

"Well, Punch," he said, "we've got work to do."

He reached up and flicked off the light above the bench. The shadows scurried eagerly out of hiding as the two started together toward the stairs.

8

PUNCH AND JUDY

II

Enter JUDY.

JUDY: Where's the baby?

PUNCH: The baby?

JUDY: Yes—our darling child.

PUNCH: Oh, *that* baby. You mean you didn't catch him?

JUDY: Catch him? Did you throw him down the stairs?

PUNCH: No—I threw him out the window. I thought you might be passing.

JUDY: Oh, you cruel, horrid man! How could you?

Exit JUDY.

PUNCH: Don't weep, my love. I promise I won't do it again.

Reenter JUDY *with stick.*

JUDY: I'll teach you to drop my baby out the window (*hits him over the head with the stick*).

PUNCH: So-o-o-ftly, Judy, so-o-o-ftly (*rubbing the back of his head*). A joke's a joke.

JUDY: Oh you nasty (*hit*) cruel (*hit*) man (*hit*). I'll teach you.

PUNCH: Please, Judy. I don't think I like your teaching. Your lessons are too hard. Stop it, will you?

JUDY: No (*hit*) I (*hit*) won't (*hit*).

PUNCH: Well, then, let's see how you like my teaching (*snatches the stick and hits her once; she drops to the ground, dead*).

There now. If you're satisfied, so am I (*sees that she doesn't move*). (*aside*) She's sulking. Get up, Judy, my dear. Enough of your games. What? Have you got a headache, then? Are you asleep? This is no time for a nap, my dear.

GHOST *rises.*

GHOST: O-o-o-o-o-o-o-o.

PUNCH (*frightened*): A-aaah.

GHOST: O-o-o-o-o-o.

PUNCH: Aaaa-ah-ah (*trembles like a leaf*).

GHOST: O-o-o-o-o-o.

PUNCH *faints.*

Exit GHOST *with* JUDY.

PUNCH (*feebly*): I'm feeling very ill. Call for a doctor, someone.

9

"OKAY—PRETEND I'M THE MOMMY and you're the little girl."

"Lela, listen to me. I'm sitting here at my desk, my book is open, my eyes are going back and forth across the page. I'm trying to read—understand?"

Lela listened. "And pretend I'm going to have a baby," she chattered on, regardless. "Pretend that it's coming really soon."

It was hopeless, utterly hopeless.

"Lela, please, I don't want to play right now. Maybe later, okay?"

"You're mean. Aunt Emily plays with me."

"Well, Aunt Emily's out right now, and I'm busy, so you'll just have to play by yourself for a while."

"No." She stamped a high-heeled foot on the floor, and almost fell flat on her face.

For the past fifteen minutes, while Alice was trying vainly to penetrate Miss Witherspoon's book on puppetry, Lela had been rummaging busily through the dress-up box, dragged out from under the bed.

She had pulled on an old plaid skirt of Mother's over her pants and a blue bouclé sweater over her shirt. On her head she wore a flaming pink tube top that looked a whole lot better as a hat than it ever had as a top. An old baby blanket, folded, served as a shawl.

As she stood there teetering with indignation in a pair of Mother's cast-off high heels, one hand held in place the doll that she had tucked up under the skirt. Two limp cloth legs hung below the hem. The baby was definitely coming very soon.

Alice took one look at her standing there swallowed up in those giant clothes, the tears welling in her wide eyes— and her heart melted. She closed the book and pushed it away.

"Okay—you're the mommy and I'm the little girl. Mommy, I think you'd better call the doctor; the baby's coming."

Lela saw the stray legs dangling below the skirt. "No," she said, quickly tucking them up out of sight. "It's not time yet. First we have to have breakfast. What do you want for breakfast, little girl?" She wiped away her tears with the back of her hand and wobbled off to the wooden stove.

For all Aunt Emily's strangeness, Alice had to admit that having her around was an enormous help. Mother was simply not able to manage on her own. The least exertion threatened to bring on the bleeding again. With the specter of losing the baby hanging over her, she was content to let her sister take control. Aunt Emily pampered her with countless cups of tea, let her do what light work she was able, and kept her tucked in bed a good deal of the time. The color had begun to return to Mother's cheeks, and she waddled cautiously around the house like a plump porcelain Buddha apt to break.

The change in Lela since her aunt had arrived on the scene had been nothing short of miraculous. The two of them were practically inseparable. Lela loved nothing better than to be read to, and Aunt Emily loved nothing better than to read. They were a perfect pair. Books followed them like flies around the house.

The family library, such as it was, consisted of a sparse

collection of paperbacks on the shelf below the television: a dozen dog-eared spy thrillers that Father had labored his way through over the past few years, all of which he swore were destined to become classics; and a pristine row of period romances with blushingly steamy covers, which Mrs. Morrison consumed like candy and passed on to Mother when she was through. It had taken Aunt Emily barely a week to bore her way through them all.

After that she began to make the occasional foray out to her car, returning with armloads of books unearthed from the junk in the backseat. It was as though they were quietly spawning out there at the heart of the chaos.

Most were library rejects in slack plastic covers, scooped up at sales in her travels around the country. She was wide and indiscriminate in her reading. One day it would be a book of Romantic poetry, the next a supernatural thriller. As long as it was print confined between covers, it captured her and carried her away.

Honored above the rest, however, was an old leather-bound, gilt-edged volume of Shakespeare. It quickly became a fixture around the house. Wherever Aunt Emily happened to be, it could not be far behind.

One morning last week Alice had wandered downstairs to discover Lela sitting on the couch with Asha clutched in her arms, while Aunt Emily read to her from the book. The vacuum cleaner had been abandoned nearby. With Aunt Emily, the housework lurched along in fits and starts.

Lela sat wide-eyed, no doubt without a clue as to what was going on, simply content to be lulled by the rhythm of the words. Alice herself had stopped at the foot of the stairs to listen. But when Aunt Emily grew aware of her, she blushed and quickly closed the book.

She was definitely a very peculiar person, extremely shy and secretive in her ways. Yet the longer she was with them, the more Alice found herself drawn to her.

One sensed that at some time something inside her had taken a slight twist, sending her down paths not normally traveled, shrouding her in mystery. Even her going out today had been mysterious—sudden, unexpected, somehow tinged with urgency.

As she'd stood at the window watching the old car lurch into life and carry her aunt off down the street, Alice had been sorely tempted to tiptoe up to the middle room and rummage around a little, convinced that she would uncover there some vital clue. Only the omnipresence of Lela stopped her. Still, the seed had been planted.

"Here's your breakfast, little girl." Lela set a small plastic plate and cup in front of her, and alongside them a spoon. The cup contained a dented Ping-Pong ball. Alice had had this breakfast before.

"Mmm, soft-boiled egg—my favorite."

Under Lela's watchful eye, she took the spoon and tapped it against the side of the ball. She detached the imaginary top of the egg and laid it on the plate.

"Just right," she said. "Nice and runny the way I like it. You make good eggs, Mommy. Did you make me some toast to dip in it?"

"Yes, little girl, " said Lela, hoisting up the doll under her skirt a little. "It's right there on your plate."

"Oh yes, I couldn't see it for a moment."

"I cut it into soldiers the way you like."

"You're such a good mommy." Alice lifted one of the imaginary fingers of toast and dunked it in the imaginary egg, then pretended to eat it. The trouble with living with Lela was that the line between reality and imagination began to blur seriously; she could almost taste the yolk-soaked finger of toast going down.

"Mmm, delicious," she said. And she thought Aunt Emily was strange.

"Good. Hurry up and eat your breakfast now, little girl. The baby's coming. It's going to come any minute now." She tottered off hurriedly toward the bed.

"Yes, Mommy, I'll hurry."

Alice felt for another of the fingers of toast, picked it up, and dunked it up and down in the runny yolk.

Cigarettes—filthy habit. She had succumbed to the old temptation and picked up a pack at the convenience store across the street from the town house development where she had parked the car. She sat in the car now, lighting the third in the half hour she had been there, opening the window to clear the smoke.

The cigarettes had been intended to calm her, to still the rising tide of fear she felt inside. All they had succeeded in doing was making her feel sick.

Emily got out of the car, closed the door, and began slowly walking along the street, feeling curiously like a foreigner in a place that had once been as familiar to her as the back of her hand.

The development was bordered by a low brick wall scarred by graffiti. Several spindly trees, swaddled in burlap and propped between metal poles, stood sentinel before it, waving their sparse leathery leaves in the wind. Here and there the wall was broken by a brick walk that trailed off into the interior of the project. It was the sort of place one might readily become lost in, a bewildering maze of houses, each much the same as the next.

There was about it an uneasy sense of menace. One felt

it in the general air of neglect that hung about the place: the garbage strewn about, the grass gone brown, the graffiti scrawled on the wall. It was the type of place that had looked like a dream on paper, and once the last brick was in place had quickly turned to nightmare.

She was not surprised. But it was not the building, not the tenants caught in its smothering embrace. It was something about the site itself. For deep underground, buried beneath countless tons of fill, there ran the remnant of a stream, doggedly channeling its way through the dark. Thirty years ago that stream had snaked across the floor of the ravine that had stood here then—a ragged swath of wilderness that cut the town in two, the final remnant of the great forest that had once covered the whole region. All that remained of it now was the tongue of trees that lay behind her sister's house.

To her child's eyes then it had been an abode of wonder and terror. Even now she could see it, as if superimposed upon this place now—a reality more powerful, somehow more present to her than this. She could see the scrub-grass lot running from the sidewalk to the edge of the ravine, the billboard standing with one foot planted on the lip and the other anchored in the depths, the bridge spanning the stream, the rusted railway tracks on the far side. And perched upon the edge of the ravine itself, the old railway depot her father had been renovating that summer a lifetime ago.

The thought of her father brought with it a sharp, sudden pang of guilt and loss that nearly twenty years had not dulled. He was gone, hopelessly and irretrievably lost to her. He had died while she was off on the other side of the country, in the midst of that long and, she knew, futile flight from fear.

Gone too was the depot, the place he had so passionately loved and she so passionately come to dread. She could picture it still, perched on the brink of the green abyss, its conical roof like a witch's cap, the two narrow windows in its waiting room like eyes shuttered in sleep.

And then one fateful night twenty-eight summers ago it had awakened, and its waking had altered the whole of her life.

She flicked the cigarette onto the sidewalk, crushed it dead with the toe of her shoe. She ought to have been glad, she supposed, glad that it was gone, obliterated, buried forever in the green dark below. She ought to have been glad— but she was not. For as certainly as she knew that somewhere deep underground there ran a river that would not be stilled, she knew that sometimes the dead did not stay buried.

It had been a breech birth, but luckily without any of the complications that can often arise when one comes feet first into the world.

Mother and child were resting comfortably in the bottom bunk. The baby, wrapped in a blanket, was pressed to its mother's breast. The strain of labor had not noticeably slowed Mother down.

"There, baby, you have a nice big drink now."

The pink bouclé sweater was balled up around Lela's armpits. Her flat bare belly rose and fell. She positioned the doll over the nipple. The doll looked curiously desperate, its permanently puckered mouth pressed to Lela's nonexistent breast, its eyes wide with alarm.

"There. She drank up all my milk. Pretend she wants to drink your milk now."

"Wait a minute, I thought I was the doctor." Alice knelt at the bedside, the toy stethoscope around her neck. Lela handed her the baby.

"That's okay. Doctors can have milk too."

"Well, pretend this doctor doesn't have any, okay?" She laid the doll down in the vacated crib by the bed and covered it carefully with a blanket. The broken eye remained open, staring vacantly up at the ceiling. Alice reached out a finger and quietly urged it closed.

10

PUNCH AND JUDY

III

Enter DOCTOR.

DOCTOR: Bless me, who's this? My good friend Mr. Punch. Poor man, how pale he looks. I'll feel his pulse (*takes* PUNCH's *arm*). One, two, fourteen, nine, eleven. Mr. Punch, are you dead?

PUNCH (*sitting up and hitting him on the nose*): Yes. (*He drops back down.*)

DOCTOR (*rubbing his nose*): I've never heard a dead man speak before. Mr. Punch, you're not dead.

PUNCH: Oh, yes I am (*hitting him as before*).

DOCTOR: How long have you been dead?

PUNCH: About six weeks, I should say.

DOCTOR: Oh, you're not dead. You're only poorly. Tell me, where does it hurt? Is it here? (*touching head*)

PUNCH: No, lower.

DOCTOR: Here?

PUNCH: No, lower, lower.

DOCTOR (*feeling him on the leg*): Here then?

PUNCH: No, lower. (*As* DOCTOR *leans over* PUNCH's *foot,* PUNCH *kicks him in the eye.*)

DOCTOR: Oh, my eye, my eye. I'll tell you what, Mr. Punch; I must go and get you some medicine.

Exit DOCTOR.

PUNCH: A fine doctor, to come without medicine.

Reenter DOCTOR *with stick. Hits* PUNCH *on the head.*

PUNCH: Oh, Doctor, what sort of medicine do you call that?

DOCTOR: Stick licorice (*hitting him*). Extract of balsam.

PUNCH: Stop! Stop! Give me the medicine in my own hands. I'll take it myself (*grabs stick and hits* DOCTOR). There, see how you like your medicine yourself.

DOCTOR: Oh me, Punch, mercy. Pay me my fee and let me go.

PUNCH: What's your fee?

DOCTOR: Five pounds.

PUNCH: Would a penny do?

DOCTOR: No. I must have nothing less than five pounds.

PUNCH: Very well then, here they are (*hits* DOCTOR). One, two, three, four, five (DOCTOR *falls down and does not move*). There, the bill is settled—and the doctor is, too, by the look of it.

11

EMILY RANG THE BELL ON THE counter a second time. An old woman hunched over a newspaper in the reading room looked up and scowled.

The marble floor was flecked with motes of colored light, like petals scattered on a pool. She glanced up. High overhead the stained-glass dome gleamed with sunlight.

At first there appeared to be no pattern to the glass. But as she studied it with growing fascination, the dark lines of leading that branched throughout seemed to sprout thorns, the random shards of color to cluster into lush, elaborate blooms. Thick buds of brilliant red seemed ready to erupt into flower.

The panic, as always, started in her stomach, as if some savage fist had buried itself in her flesh. For one horrific moment the air was heavy with the odor of roses.

"May I help you?"

She whirled and for an instant saw a gleeful white face glaring down at her. The image vanished, leaving in its wake a lean young man in a white smock standing at the counter.

"Sorry to keep you waiting," he said. "I was over in the children's section doing a bit of painting. What can I do for you?"

He was looking at her strangely. She struggled to gather herself together, to regain control—and found herself addressing the floor.

"I was told that the Railway Museum is now housed in

67

the library. Is that so?" She forced herself to look him in the eyes.

"Yes, though I'm afraid there's not much left. There was a fire, you see. It—"

"Yes—I know."

This time it was he who turned away.

"Could you tell me where it is kept?" she asked, eager to end the conversation.

"Yes. Upstairs." His eyes traveled to the marble railing around the rotunda at the upper level. "In the west wing. There are several display cases by the window."

"Thank you."

"I could show—"

"Thank you, I'll be fine."

She felt his eyes on her all the way up the wide, winding staircase. The marble railing felt sepulchral against her palm. Her body had turned to ice. If she stumbled now she was sure she would shatter into countless glistening shards.

An unnerving stillness pervaded the upper floor. There was no one else about. Her feet whispered against the wooden floor as she made her way around the rotunda to the room.

It was a large, high-ceilinged room, the lower portion of the walls paneled in the rich dark wood of the furnishings: two long tables with chairs, four freestanding ranges of bookshelves running the length of the room. A large stone fireplace with a mantelpiece of the same wood stood against the wall to her left. Pre-Raphaelite prints lined the walls above the wainscoting. Women with flesh like ivory and hair like burnished gold. It was a room forgotten by time.

Her eye wandered down one of the narrow aisles between the rows of books to the high mullioned windows on the far wall. Standing dwarfed beneath them she saw the small metal display cases that her father had purchased for the museum. They struck the only jarring note in the room, clearly intruders from another time.

She could still picture her father busy in the basement, painting them in the brilliant blue and yellow calling colors of the Niagara Northwestern Railway Line. She noticed that the corner of one case had been blackened somewhat by the fire—that mysterious fire that had so conveniently destroyed the building and cleared the way for the developers.

Her father had never really recovered from the loss. It was just six months afterward that he had had the first in the series of heart attacks that would carry him off less than a year later.

And this was all that remained now of his life's labor—six squat metal cases tucked away in a time-forgotten room. She stood before the first of them now, feeling forgotten by time herself, fighting back the old anguish, fighting down the old fear. She ran her finger through the dust that had gathered on the glass.

Inside, faded posters, old timetables, ticket stubs, a lump of soil in a tarnished silver box. All neatly labeled in her father's hand.

The next case was full of photographs, also labeled: the arrival of the first train in town, smoke pluming from its stack, the depot decked out in bunting, the platform full of people; interior shots from the same period of the stationmaster's office and the circular waiting room, the wood stove in the center of the room, benches built into the wall; still others of the station through the years, the silent chronicle of its slow decline to the boarded-up, abandoned relic she remembered as a child. She had seen them all before.

In one corner of the case, though, were two photographs she hadn't seen before. They were labeled Opening Day Celebrations, Caledon Railway Museum. The first was a formal shot; it showed a group gathered on the platform of the newly renovated depot. The mayor of the day, along with several other dignitaries, stood front and center, smiling. To either side of them stood the members of the Historical Society, among them her father in his Sunday suit, smiling awkwardly out at her. He looked so young, yet he had seemed ancient to her then. She realized with a shock that he had been no older then than she was now.

The other photo was an interior shot, taken on the same day. It showed a crowd milling about the waiting room, looking at the displays. Again she saw her father, this time standing before the large model train layout he had constructed, depicting the town at the turn of the century. Beside him was her younger brother, Albert, looking angelic. But as her eyes scanned the picture, they settled on two figures in the background, a girl and an older woman standing together before one of the display cases. Both were looking toward the camera. She was the girl. The woman was Irma Potts.

One glance and she was instantly cast back to that September day twenty-eight years ago. Then, as now, she had wandered as in a dream from case to case. But with someone on her arm then, supporting her, strengthening her. Dear Miss Potts, gone now too. And she left here alone, to watch and wait.

He will be back, won't he?

Yes, my dear, I believe he will be back.

She forced her feet along to the next case, feeling like one in a morgue, moving mechanically from box to box, dreading that the next would frame the missing face. She forced herself to look down.

And there it was. Some part of her had known all along that it would be here, that if the whole exhibit had been consumed by fire, it would have survived.

It lay there in the dusty case among the other relics of a vanished age, a poster for a magic show, in two brittle halves upon the felt, flaked and yellowed with age. To anyone else it would have seemed a quaint curiosity, hardly more interesting than the crumbling lump of sod. To her, however, it was the emblem of terror.

PROFESSOR MEPHISTO
PRESENTS . . .
AN EVENING OF MAGIC AND MYSTERY.

Her eyes traveled down the list of illusions to be performed—the Mysterious Portfolio, the Ethereal Suspension, the Vanishing Lady, the Decollation of John the Baptist—each one sounding its solemn knell inside her, each one coming loose like the futile nails on a coffin lid, as something stirred inside.

Sometimes the dead do not stay buried.

And there, near the bottom of the playbill, the program date—Saturday, August 8.

It rang in her ears like thunder. The very room seemed to thrum with it, and darkness whistled down her spine. A lilting voice sounded in her ear, the voice that visited her dreams every night now. And again she saw the gleeful white face of the magician staring down at her from the stage.

Yes, you by the door. Do come in, dear. Don't be shy. There's much more yet to come.

It was as though he stood beside her now. She whirled and scanned the empty room. She wanted to run, wanted to run from this building, jump behind the wheel of her car and flee this place forever.

But she could not. She had come back—and here she must stay. She felt so small, so utterly small and insignificant, impossibly unsuited to the overwhelming task that lay before her.

She turned to go. But as she turned, something in the next case caught her eye and stopped her dead in her tracks. She approached it haltingly. Among the other items in the case was a knife—a knife with a long curved blade and jewel-encrusted hilt.

One glance at it lying there quietly on its bed of felt and the blood froze in her veins.

Mother spread the mustard lovingly over the salami, licked the knife, then set it down on her plate. She settled the top half of the bun back on the sandwich.

"I feel deliciously delinquent," she said as she brought it to her mouth.

Alice, who was perched on the edge of the bed leafing through the latest batch of books she had brought home for her mother from the library, looked up and smiled. Mother had been reading everything on pregnancy she could lay her hands on. The entire childbirth section of Parkview Public was housed now in her room.

"I'd almost forgotten what meat tasted like. Where did you get this from anyway?"

"Father has emergency supplies stashed away in the basement fridge. I caught him creeping down there last night after Aunt Emily had gone to bed."

"I might have known. That was very thoughtful of you to bring me up some lunch. What's Lela up to?"

"She's having a little nap. We had a busy morning; she delivered three babies in less than an hour."

Mother almost choked on her sandwich. "You're kidding?"

"No. And it would have been four if the doctor hadn't gone on strike." She leafed through one of the books on the bed—pages of full-color photographs following the development of the child in the womb. It was incredible.

"How on earth did they take these pictures?"

Mother leaned over to look. "I'm not exactly sure. I think they mounted a miniature camera lens on the end of a surgical probe and somehow inserted it into the uterus."

"Sounds delightful."

"Here, let me see it. I'll show you where we are now." She began to flip through the book. A spot of mustard stained the corner of her mouth.

"Here we are. Thirty weeks. We're just a little further along than this."

The picture showed a figure draped as in a veil, its eyes shut, its finger tucked securely in its mouth.

"Boy, it's hard to believe that that little creature is in here," said Mother, feeling her belly. "You know, it's strange, but with you and Lela I never really thought about it much; it just sort of happened. But with this one—maybe because we've come so close to losing it—I think of it all the time. I'm even trying to talk your father into helping me through the labor. The doctor seems to think it would be a good idea, too."

"And what does Dad have to say about it?"

"Well, let's just say it's a long way from the waiting room to the labor room; we're working on it." She smiled and took another bite of the sandwich. "Still no sign of Emily, I guess?"

"No."

"Did she say where she was going?"

"No, just that there was something she had to do."

"Well, that's Emily. She wraps herself in mystery. It's her element. Your grandfather used to call her the Enigma. She's very good at heart, though. How are you getting on with her?"

"Fine, I guess. She's a little—I don't know—strange."

"Yes, I suppose she is. I guess we're all a little strange in our own way."

"Was she always like that, then?"

"No, not always. She was actually quite ordinary once. When we were young, being the eldest of the bunch, she was called upon to help out quite a bit. Especially after my little brother Albert was born. In some ways she was almost like a second mother to us. Oh, there were times when I could cheerfully have murdered her. But that's to be expected, I suppose.

"It wasn't until she was into her teens that she began to change. She had this teacher in grade eight—what was her name, now? Oh, never mind, it'll come to me. Before that I don't remember her being particularly bookish at all. But after that year, well, she became very serious all of a sudden, very, I don't know, internal. Potts, that was the teacher's name: Miss Potts."

Alice started. She remembered the inscription in the *Wonder Book*: "Irma Potts 1931. Grandma gave it to me."

"Now there was a strange woman for you," her mother continued. "I never had her myself, mind you. She'd retired before I got to grade eight. But, believe me, her reputation lived on.

"She used to talk to herself, they said. Talked to her plants, too. And she was a demon for poetry. She'd recite

74

long passages of Shakespeare to her classes from memory. Oh, she was definitely a case, all right.

"Anyway, Emily had her this one year. And the summer after that they saw quite a lot of each other, I remember. I could never figure out why. After that summer Emily was never really the same again." She paused for a moment, massaging her giant stomach through the sheets, lost in thought. "Lord, it's been a long time since I thought of all this.

"Miss Potts died a few years later. Emily was out of town at college by then, but she came back for the funeral and stayed at the house with us. She was like a stranger. She didn't even look like the Emily I'd grown up with. She'd become thin, even thinner than she is now. She was very much the artist—distant, preoccupied, practically unapproachable. It was soon afterward that she published her first book of poetry."

Alice looked up, interested. "I didn't know she wrote poetry."

"Oh yes, she's done two or three books. I've got them tucked away somewhere. Anyway, that was the last time she was in Caledon until now, for that funeral. And that was more than twenty years ago.

"Oh, she's always written to us, as you know; she's a very faithful letter writer, much better than I, I'm afraid. And she's always had a special place in her heart for Albert. But she's never really settled, for some reason. It's as if she somehow can't settle. Well, you know how she is with that room."

It was true; Father had offered countless times since Aunt Emily's arrival to make over the baby's room for her while she was staying with them—take down the crib, bring up the foldaway bed from the basement, empty out the drawers of the white dresser for her things. The answer was always the same: she wouldn't hear of it.

"Bad enough luck putting the crib up before the baby's come," she'd say. "I won't risk worse by having you take it down on my account."

And so she continued to bed down in her sleeping bag on the rug.

"But you can't possibly be comfortable on the floor," Mother had lamented one night last week.

"I'm perfectly comfortable. Perfectly."

"Is that why you're up half the night then?"

"I'm 'up half the night,' as you say, Elizabeth, because I do my best thinking at night. If I slept the night away, I'm sure my brain would shrivel up like a lemon rind. And if you were sleeping—as you should be—you wouldn't hear me, would you?"

"You are a very frustrating woman, Emily."

"So I'm told."

And so she remained with them, like a bird perched on a bough, apt in an instant to take flight.

Alice made tiny tucks in the sheet as she sat on the edge of the bed. Was that what Aunt Emily was up to in the room every night then? Writing poetry?

"Mom, you wouldn't know offhand where those books are, would you?"

"You mean Emily's poetry? I think I do. Why, would you like to look at them?"

"Yes, I would." Her mother's glance was probing; she met it briefly, then looked back to the sheet.

"I think they're in the cedar chest. Have a look if you'd like."

The cedar chest was a family heirloom, Mother's most

prized possession. It sat in all its antique splendor at the foot of the bed. Once, Lela had made the mistake of using it as a springboard to jump onto the bed. She hadn't made that mistake twice.

The warm, rich odor of the wood greeted Alice as she opened the lid. Stacks of lace doilies, runners, tablecloths too cherished to risk using, a faded silk kimono swathed in tissue paper, a smiling portrait of Grandfather in a cracked frame, Mother and Father's white wedding album, and boxes of family photographs—all of them redolent of cedar.

"There's a box of letters there on the left," said Mother, invisible behind the open lid. "A blue satin box. Do you see it?"

"Yes."

"Those are Emily's letters. I think the books are under them."

Alice opened the box. There must have been well over a hundred letters, envelopes of every shape and size, all of them bearing the stamp of Aunt Emily's unmistakable scrawl, as if a bird with inked feet had sauntered across the paper. She lifted a handful out and caught a glimpse of something green on the bottom of the box.

"Yes, here they are, I think." She reached in and came out with three thin clothbound books. Stray letters spilled into the chest. She retrieved them, tucked them along with the others back into the box, then closed the lid of the chest.

"Yes, that's them." Mother took one last bite of the sandwich and set the tray aside.

Alice leafed through one of the books. Forty-five numbered poems on cream-colored ragged-edged paper. The title tooled on the spine was *A Rumor of Roses*. On the title page there was an inscription. She was struggling to make sense of the impossible scrawl when she was startled by a light knock on the door. It edged open.

In came Aunt Emily, carrying a tray.

"Oh, I'm sorry. Am I interrupting?"

"No, not at all, Emily. I didn't realize you were back."

"I thought you might like a little—" Her eyes fell on the remains of the salami sandwich.

Mother flushed. "Oh, Alice brought me up a little something."

"I see." Her face stiffened slightly; she shifted her gaze to Alice, now standing by the bed with the books.

"Alice didn't realize you wrote," explained Mother, obviously uncomfortable. "I was just showing her your books."

"I didn't know you'd kept them." She put the tray down on the edge of the bed: apple slices, a piece of cheese, a buttered bun. Alice noticed that one of her hands was bandaged.

"Why, of course I kept them. I've read every one too."

Emily looked at her—didn't say a word, just looked. Her face appeared paler than usual. She seemed distracted.

"You haven't published anything recently, have you?" said Mother, trying bravely to bridge the silence.

"No." It was a no meant to put an end to all conversation. Alice found herself wishing she were shut in the cedar chest with the lace tablecloths.

"Oh, you've hurt yourself," said Mother. "What happened?"

"It's nothing," Emily said, whisking the bandaged hand behind her back. "A little accident. I'd better go. I've got the water on for tea."

She drifted out the door like a ghost. There was a quiet click as it closed, then silence. Alice waited for the telling creak of stairs.

"See what I mean," she said. "Strange."

12

THE MURAL COVERED THE UPPER third of one wall in the Children's Room. It depicted a forest scene: dreamlike, idyllic. Tall, stately trees rose like marble columns to a canopy of green; here and there a sudden shaft of light filtered through and discovered in the shadows of the trees a group of children, unseen at first amid the towering trunks. They leaned against the trees and lounged on the ground, their eyes wide with wonder.

The object of that wonder was a woman, half hidden by the shadows; in her hand an open book caught one of the random shafts of light that lit the scene. She was reading from the book, standing majestically among the trees with one arm extended slightly and the book cradled in her outstretched hand.

She wore a white dress belted at the waist. It and the clothes the children wore seemed somehow out of place in the scene. It was as if the forest had risen magically around them while she read.

The mural was as old as the library itself. Time had darkened the dream it depicted, lent shadows to the faces among the trees, flaked bits of leaf and flesh away to expose the bare plaster beneath. Despite this, though, it retained its magic, and regardless of the passage of time and all the many changes it had wrought, those children still sat spellbound in the wonder of that moment among the trees.

Alice, her head arched back, tried yet again to make out the murky features of the woman in the mural—and rammed into a wastebasket with her cart of books. The dream dissolved in a tinny thud and a scattering of crushed paper across the floor. The little girl reading at the desk jumped about a foot in the air, then quickly scrambled down to help Alice gather the stuff back into the can. She had obviously had a nosebleed; bits of bloody tissue plugged her nose. She refused to make eye contact as she scooped up the soiled tissue, barely nodding her head in acknowledgment when Alice asked if she was all right. As soon as they were finished she slid quietly back into her seat and melted instantly back into her book.

The laughter that had erupted from a neighboring table where a couple of boys were playing checkers had subsided, and they were suddenly intent on their game as Alice pushed the squeaking cart past them, pausing to scoop up an abandoned book on the way.

It was five-fifteen, cleanup time before the six o'clock Friday closing. Back home Aunt Emily would be setting her vegetable-sodden brain to work on what to make for dinner, sifting through the cupboards for clues, doggedly ignoring the freezerful of assorted meats swaddled in pink butcher paper, which Father just as doggedly continued to cart home, letting her eye light rather on the half tub of tofu soaking in its water bath on the rack below the milk. Mother would be curled up on the couch reading, one hand resting on her stomach, waiting for the quiet reassurance of a kick.

Here, though most of the tables were occupied, about the only ones really reading were the little girl with the nosebleed and the mysterious woman in the mural. The rest were simply killing time until their parents got home from work.

The closest most of these kids came to a book were the rock portfolios available at the desk along with the games, or the tattered teen magazines lying ravaged on the racks.

At one table a group of girls, their lips all painted the

same lurid red, gathered around a magazine opened to a glossy picture of a moon-faced boy with a shock of blond hair falling over one eye. They gave Alice the once-over as she squeaked by with the cart, and broke into smothered giggles behind her back. Obviously she had failed the test.

Two boys at a nearby table, with paperbacks strewn around them like fallen leaves, brooded over a large book opened between them while keeping one eye fixed intently on the girls. As Alice gathered up the stray books on the table and heaped them on top of the already overflowing cart, she glanced down at the object of their interest; it was a glossy history of military weaponry. Girls and guns; to see the two so closely twinned was somehow terrifying.

Conversations carried on behind the blinds of books subsided as she approached, then started up again in her wake. At some of the tables children sat alone; these were the obvious pariahs, somehow different than the rest, ragged, remote, their dark eyes intent on the clock or the view of the woods out the window.

How different those woods from the woods in the mural hovering over them all. How different these tough, brittle children from those nestled quietly among the painted trees.

Alice pushed the cart over to the seclusion of the window seat and began unloading the books onto the bench, setting them in order before reloading the cart.

A cough nearby caught her attention. Curled in one corner of the picture-book alcove she saw a small girl bent over a book, her hair hanging like curtains to either side of her face, hiding it from sight. She reminded her strangely of Lela, a Lela three or four years down the road. She did not seem quite real somehow, hunched intently over her book, hidden from the rest of the room. It was as though she had descended from the mural on the wall above.

Someone was banging on the service bell at the front desk. The spell shattered like glass. Alice set down the armload of books she was sorting. There was no sign of Mr. Dwyer. Since school had ended and she had begun working four full days a week, she noticed that he seemed to be distancing himself more and more from the daily fray, letting those duties fall to her, while he spent long stretches of time closeted in his office working on the play.

He had decided that the first step toward performing it was to transcribe the text and make copies for each of them. That would give them something concrete to start from. He spent hours poring over the old manuscript, pecking it out painstakingly at the typewriter, seemingly oblivious of all else.

The woman waiting at the desk made no attempt to mask her irritation at being forced to wait. Alice signed out her books with a smile. The three girls were gathered around the ancient photocopy machine now, making multiple copies of the moon-faced boy for their personal use. Momentarily they would make their way over to the counter to complain about the thick black band that the machine was doubtless slapping down the center of the sheet, as it had been doing all afternoon. The thought of having to face their righteous indignation was just too much. She took the coward's course and deserted her post.

Mr. Dwyer was sitting in his office. The order he had so passionately imposed upon the chaos Miss Witherspoon had left behind had begun to erode. A large stack of mail lay unopened on one corner of the desk. Three or four piles of books, each with their individual traumas to be attended to, languished in another corner. Half a dozen of the boxed puppet sets they had lugged up from the basement almost two weeks ago now, to be inventoried and cataloged, sat untouched on the floor in front of the desk where they had been left. The mustiness they had brought up with them now permeated the room.

He turned from the typewriter as she came in. "Ah, Alice, I've just finished typing the text. I was wondering if you could stay awhile tonight after closing. There are some things we should go over."

He gave her one of those strange fixed smiles of his. There was an unnerving intensity in his eyes. She felt for a moment as if she were looking at a stranger.

"All right," she said, hating herself instantly for having agreed. "Just for a while." The bell sounded again. "I'd better get back."

"Yes. I'll be along in a few minutes to give you a hand."

By the time he emerged five minutes later he had metamorphosed. He had put on his jacket and combed his hair. The wildness had drained from his eyes. She found herself wondering if she had simply imagined it. He was cheerful with the customers, coddling the old women, hurrying the kids along.

As they were busy signing out books for the last few patrons, an old gentleman who regularly worked in the local history section upstairs came down and called Mr. Dwyer aside. There were a few whispered words, then Mr. Dwyer hurried off upstairs alone.

The last customer was out the door and she had locked up and drawn the blinds when he called to her from the top of the stairs. She went up and followed him into the large room in the west wing. It was a room rarely used.

"There appears to have been some damage done to one of the display cases," he explained as he led her over to the museum displays by the window. The glass top of one of the cases had been shattered. Shards of glass littered the felt inside.

"Something seems to have been taken." There was a patch of felt free of glass, the outline of a missing object. Mr. Dwyer reached into the case and brushed aside fragments of glass that covered a small descriptive card. He took it out, read it, and passed it to her.

"Ornamental knife," she read. "Eighteenth century. Discovered on the site of the depot during demolition."

"You know," said Mr. Dwyer, "the odd thing is that just yesterday a woman came in asking about the collection. A rather odd woman."

As he began to describe his encounter with the woman, Alice found herself listening with growing disbelief. Aunt Emily? No, it couldn't be. What possible reason could she have for doing such a thing? Yet the description was dead on; how many more of her could there be? Again she saw her whisk the bandaged hand behind her back.

"I'll have to report this to the police," she heard Mr. Dwyer say, then listened numbly to the sound of his fading footsteps echo through the empty room.

13

A WEEK HAD PASSED SINCE THE discovery of the broken case. The police had dutifully come, filled out their reports, and disappeared. The shattered glass had been swept away, and the insurance company had paid for its replacement. The old man who had reported the damage had resumed his research on the growth of industry in the town of Caledon in the nineteenth century. The sun shone down on his desk as he worked, and shone too on the new glass in the small display case beneath the window. The incident had begun already to recede into memory. Nothing remained of it now but the faint outline of a missing object on the felt within the case, and a small hand-lettered card below it describing an ornamental knife. Of the mysterious woman, no more had been heard.

The week had brought with it a wave of stifling heat, which had settled over the city like a shroud. With the heat had come that creeping demon of anxiety, which in those susceptible to its influence had lodged like a lump of darkness at the base of the skull, filling the days with vague feelings of dread and the nights with ominous dreams.

Lela, of course, was immune to it all. She took to the heat like a tropical flower; blooming riotously beneath the unremitting sun, closing abruptly in the dark, exhaling the sweet perfume of sweat through the night as she slept deep and undisturbed.

The upstairs of the house was like an oven. The air was thick, glutinous, and the fan did nothing but stir the soup around.

The night before, while creeping into bed, Alice had stumbled over Asha in the dark, and in a fit of anger, brought on no doubt by the unrelenting heat, had flung the doll against the wall.

It was a totally futile gesture; she had lain in the top bunk for close to an hour, utterly unable to fall asleep, until finally she climbed down, rescued the doll from where it lay on its back by the desk, and quietly brought it up to bed with her.

Along with it she brought the flashlight from the top drawer of the desk and one of the three thin books of poetry. They had lain as undisturbed in the desk drawer since the day she borrowed them as they had in the cedar chest before then. The gnawing conviction that her aunt was in fact the mysterious woman in the library was enough to make her wary about venturing further into the darkness that enveloped the woman. She sensed that something more than stray dolls might lie lurking there.

Asha sat mutely by her in the bed while Alice trained the flashlight on the book and opened it. Mother had lied. The book had obviously never been read. The binding groaned at this sudden intrusion on its sleep. Was this then what had lain behind Aunt Emily's look?

She turned to the title page. *A Rumor of Roses* by Emily Endicott. How strange to see the name of one so secretive standing there naked on the page. She flipped to the first poem and began to read:

> *Now as the night puts forth its thorns*
> *And starbuds dot the tangled dark,*
> *We shall pass the better portion of an hour*
> *In the pain of picking roses. . . .*

Poetry was not quite her normal fare. At first it seemed difficult, deliberately obscure. But the rhythms were sure and carried her along. Soon she found herself whispering phrases aloud as she lay hunched over the book in the feeble beam of light.

She found the poems had the power to make random, vivid pictures in her mind, like sparks struck from flint. Images of childhood and old age, of nature ever changing, of birth and death, joy and pain; and binding them all like beads upon a string, a thread of magic that ran throughout. There was about them, above all, an overwhelming air of mystery, of the day to day made suddenly strange.

By the time she finally closed the book her eyes were aching with fatigue. She felt as if the room were pulsing. The night seemed suddenly alive, pregnant with unseen presences. The doll sitting beside her in the dark seemed poised on the brink of speech. She switched off the flashlight and settled under the sheets. Almost instantly she was asleep.

On the wall by the bed the wind whispered through the leaves of the wallpaper pattern. The birds fluttered fitfully on the branches. In the darkness behind them something seemed to stir.

Alice tidied up the bookcase, gathered up the toys that lay like hazards all over the floor, and finally made the beds. The slightest exertion brought on streams of sweat. From her own bed she removed the flashlight and the book of poetry. There was no sign of Asha now. She, along with a few of the other chosen, had been taken out into the yard to sunbathe by the pool.

Alice arranged the remaining dolls on their chairs

around the tea table. Their lunch had been set out for them before Lela had left, two painted wooden blocks on a plate for each of them. It was far too hot for eating, though, and the dolls sat lethargically at the table, looking limp and bedraggled. They had flung most of their clothes onto the floor.

While she folded the clothes back into the doll drawer, Alice glanced from time to time out the window into the backyard. The pool, an old tin tub liberated from its hook in the shed this morning and filled with water to be warmed by the sun, was set down near the back of the yard. There a bit of breeze blew from the woods, and the shed spread its square of shade on the grass like a handkerchief set out to dry.

Lela sat happily in that shade now, dunking Asha unceremoniously under the water, watching the frantic bubbles flutter to the surface, then lifting the doll to study the desperate stream that drained from the hole between its legs. The other dolls, no doubt thankful to have been spared the ordeal themselves, lay on a faded beach towel, baking in the heat. One of them had turned to do its back.

Aunt Emily was busy hanging out the clothes on the line. Another of her peculiarities was that she absolutely refused to have anything to do with the basement, where the washer and dryer were kept. Instead, she would do small loads of clothes in the kitchen sink several times a week and hang them out to dry. The line, which had not been used in years, had been wrenched into sudden service and had still not quite recovered. It shrieked in shock every time it was touched. It was shrieking now.

It was a little difficult getting used to the family's underwear fluttering gaily out over the yard for all to see.

Alice had taken to hoarding her own things under the bunk and doing a discreet load in the basement once a week.

She finished folding the last of the doll clothes into the drawer. The clothesline had stopped its shrieking. A quick peek out the window showed Aunt Emily and Lela sitting in a lawn chair at the back of the house, sunk quietly together in a book. They would both be utterly dead to the world for a while.

The clothes hung slack and dead in the dull heat; the sun glared off the pool; the dolls baked. Alice gathered all her resolve and stole out into the hall.

She crept down first to peek in on Mother. She lay on top of the sheets, asleep. The fan droned on the dresser, a film of sweat covered her face; the thin nightgown clung to her swollen belly. Did the baby sleep now, too? Alice wondered. And if so, did it dream?

She tiptoed down the hall to what she still thought of as the baby's room. The door was open just a touch. Through the crack she saw the small white crib, washed in sunlight, the mobile suspended motionless above it. Her stomach had knotted itself into a tight ball.

She tried to coax herself into calmness. She was just visiting the baby's room, she told herself as she gently nudged open the door. She kept her eyes fixed on the mobile and felt it draw her into the room like an errant planet suddenly caught in the pull of its field.

It was not until she was wholly inside that she dared let her eyes drift down to the sleeping bag rolled up against the wall hidden by the door, the old suitcase propped open beside it, the two cardboard boxes like bookends, books ranged along the floor between them. The *Wonder Book* from Lela's shelf lay on top of them. So this was where it had gotten to. Lela had practically torn the place apart the night before, looking for it. Strange.

There was something not quite real about the scene. The broad shaft of sunlight did not venture to this side of the room. Shadows seemed to hang about her aunt's belongings, as if a sudden shift in light might make them disappear.

On the one hand Aunt Emily was a powerful presence among them; she had stepped in and utterly altered their lives. But on another, deeper level she was like a ghost, choosing to remain almost invisible in this room rather than threaten the delicate spell under which it lay.

Alice leaned down and discovered that the old book was opened at the story of Bluebeard. And there was the terrifying picture of Bluebeard handing the ring of keys over to his new bride, giving her free use of them, yet warning her not to dare use the small key that opened the room at the end of the passage. She remembered the dreadful sight that met the eyes of the poor woman when she disobeyed the warning: the floor covered in blood, and lying in that blood the bodies of his former wives.

She closed the book and stole another look down into the yard. The two of them were still sitting together, lost in their book. She knelt down on the ground and let her eyes scan the spines of the books lined against the wall: a few old novels, a couple of poetry collections, and a curious old book on magic, *Victorian Stage Magic Illustrated*.

Up until this point she'd managed to keep herself more or less calm. If anyone should come in, she would simply say she'd been looking for the lost book. But as she lifted the flap of the first box and felt her heart begin to race, she knew she had crossed over into darker regions. There was no road back.

The box was full of clothes: underthings thrown together, faded tops, worn sweaters, a couple of pairs of pants. The woman was a walking rummage sale. Alice toyed briefly with the thought of abandoning the whole insane idea, then found herself shifting over in front of the second box.

This one was a hodgepodge, crammed with odds and ends in no discernible order: bottles of vitamin pills, creams and ointments, a safety razor in a water-stained wooden box, a bottle of perfume, still full. Down one side, a package of cigarettes had been discreetly tucked away—a secret vice. A thick book in black leather binding lay at the other end of the box along with a flashlight, extra batteries, half a dozen pencils bundled with a rubber band, and cream-colored stationery with matching envelopes of the sort she'd seen in the cedar chest.

She picked up the book and opened it. It was a journal. It had obviously been kept for a long time. The earliest entries dated back more than five years. All but the last few pages were filled with that crabbed, almost illegible scrawl that she had come to associate with Aunt Emily.

With a dreadful sense of violation she flipped to the entries that had been made since her aunt's arrival at the house. There were perhaps half a dozen pages, dated intermittently. The punctuation consisted of sharp, hurried slashes at the ends of sentences. She made out random words, phrases, none of it making much sense, but all of it evoking in her a growing sense of unease.

> July 2—He will be back, I said—Yes, she said, he will
> be back—But where will he strike? Where?
> July 8—Less than one month—Last night I heard
> his voice. I am afraid to sleep.

She was not aware of the passing of time. She did not see that the chair below the second-floor window was now empty; she did not hear the slap of the screen door downstairs.

She closed the book and was just returning it to the box when she noticed something wedged down the side where the book had been. It was wrapped in a handkerchief spotted with blood. She reached in, felt the smooth sweep of the blade through the cloth; then she heard the footsteps on the stairs.

Terror whistled down her spine. For a moment that stretched into eternity she felt herself rooted to the spot. Lela's voice echoed up the staircase, laughing. Alice's eyes swept the room frantically for escape; she leaped to her feet and launched herself toward the stack of books against the wall.

As the door opened she was standing looking down at the *Wonder Book* in her hand, the terrible eyes of Bluebeard glowering up at her from the page.

"Oh, hi," she said. "I hope you don't mind me coming into your room. I was just looking for this."

Aunt Emily's eyes flitted from her to the boxes lined against the wall. "No," she said, "not at all."

It was after midnight when the rain began, pattering against the windowpane like small ghostly fingers. Emily sat on the floor; the candle guttered in its stand beside her. Her notebook lay open on her lap, but she had not managed to work so much as a word past the anxiety that gnawed at the pit of her stomach.

She wondered if the window in the girls' room was open. If so, it would have to stay so, despite the rain. She would not risk disturbing their sleep.

Sleep. She hardly knew the meaning of the word anymore. How desperately she envied the sleep of Lela, her little one, deep and dreamless, the darkness still unknown. How she envied all of them in fact, envied them their rootedness, their innocence.

Little had she known when she came how completely she would become immersed in their lives. If she could she would encapsulate them all, close all the doors and windows on their world to the relentless drumming of fate demanding entrance.

They thought her strange. She knew that. She could read the look in Alice's eyes whenever they met. Had that same look not couched in her own eyes when Miss Potts had first confided her fears in Emily that fateful summer a lifetime ago? Had things not in fact come full circle now, she the slightly mad spinster and Alice the innocent on the edge?

How much Alice reminded her of herself at that age, so curious, so skeptical. Yet already there was that about her that spoke of a brush with darkness, the unmistakable stamp of shadow on the soul. Perhaps it was the burden of the pregnancy that lay over them all. But she sensed it was more.

Could Alice too sense the foreboding that lay in the air? Was it that which had drawn her to this room today, which had sent her rooting through her things? For there was no doubt she had been prowling; the chaos was slightly askew.

She reached down the side of the box, withdrew the knife, unwrapped it. In the dull light of the candle it appeared to glow. It possessed a power. She could almost feel it pulsing in her hand. Her finger ran along the jewels that decorated the hilt, probed the hollows where two were missing. And the unsettling thought surfaced in her mind once more. Had bringing this here somehow tempted the darkness here as well?

14

Punch and Judy

IV

Enter POLICEMAN.

POLICEMAN: Enough of your singing, Mr. Punch. I've come to make you sing out of the other side of your mouth.

PUNCH: And who the devil are you?

POLICEMAN: I am the policeman. Take your nose out of my face, sir.

PUNCH: And who sent for you? Take your face out of my nose, sir.

POLICEMAN: I'm sent for you, sir. I've a special order to lock you up for the murder of your child, your wife (*bends over* DOCTOR), and your doctor too.

PUNCH: And I've a special order to knock you down (*does so*).

POLICEMAN (*rising*): Come along now, I've a warrant for you.

PUNCH (*hitting him*): And there's a warrant for you (*knocks him down*).

POLICEMAN: Come along quietly, it's off to jail with you.

PUNCH (*kicking*): I won't go.

POLICEMAN (*shouting*): More help, more help. Be quick.

Enter JACK KETCH, *the hangman.*

96

KETCH: What's all this?

POLICEMAN: This man is resisting arrest.

KETCH (*to* PUNCH): Do you know me?

PUNCH (*with obvious alarm*): Oh, sir, I know you very well. I hope you and Mrs. Ketch are well.

KETCH: You are a wicked man. Why did you kill the doctor?

PUNCH: Self-defense. He tried to kill me.

KETCH: How?

PUNCH: With his blasted medicine.

KETCH: Nonsense. You must come along to prison now and pay for your crimes.

(*They fall on* PUNCH *and carry him off while he cries out.*)

PUNCH: "Help! Murder! Save me!"

15

THE HEAT BROKE AT LAST, AND with it went some of the anxiety that had been steadily building in the small house. The night air blew through open windows while they slept; it bore with it a faint odor of roses.

The black band that had been skulking at the bottom of the TV screen for months suddenly lunged one night and swallowed the entire screen. It proved impervious to father's pleadings and poundings. For two nights he sat in a sulk, staring into sound. Finally, he picked up the battered copy of *Six Practical Lessons for an Easier Childbirth* and began to read.

Alice tried desperately to push the events of the preceding week to the back of her mind. But she kept finding herself drawn to the upstairs room in the library, to the empty space where the knife should have been, to the crumbling playbill in the case beside it.

PROFESSOR MEPHISTO
PRESENTS . . .
AN EVENING OF MAGIC AND MYSTERY.

Something about it brought zero to the bone.

She was convinced now that Aunt Emily had seen through her awkward attempt to explain why she had been in her room, was convinced that her aunt knew full well she had been snooping, perhaps even sensed what she had been looking for. Alice could hardly bear to be in the same room with her now, for fear that she would finally confront her with it.

But why had she stolen the knife? What possible reason could she have had? Or was it a question of reason at all? The day before, Alice had wandered into the kitchen to find Aunt Emily staring fixedly at the calendar above the stove, flipping forward into the next month, then back again, as if she were counting days.

The calendar was all but clear. Months ago Mother had circled her due date, August 13, and recently Alice had noted the date of the puppet show. Beyond that it was blank. There were precious few landmarks in their lives these days. The world was on hold until the baby came.

Her aunt had turned from the stove and found her standing there. In her eyes there was a deep and almost desperate look of fear.

Alice found herself more and more frequently seeking refuge from the house in the backyard. Today when she came out after lunch to sit in the sun and read, Lela had come tumbling out after her. She headed immediately down to the sandbox with Asha under her arm and flung the screened lid unceremoniously onto the grass. It was uncanny the way she'd taken to that doll, lavishing affection on the homely thing nearly to the exclusion of the others.

Aunt Emily had played her part; one night the week before she had sat and knitted an outfit for the doll, complete with hat and bootees; she had scrubbed its rubber face in the sink with a stiff brush until the rash that covered it had been reduced to mere shadows. With the hat now hiding its stubbled hair, it looked almost sweet in a strange sort of way.

On her own, Lela had somehow managed to extricate

the old doll carriage from the shed and was busy rooting sandy dishes out from under the dolls that were crammed into it. They, obviously, had not been invited to the party. It was to be a private affair between herself and Asha.

One limp leg of the Victoria doll, draped with a few bedraggled strands of woolen hair, hung desolately over the edge of the carriage: The doll was bent double in its bed, its head wedged between its legs.

A sudden wave of guilt washed over Alice, fueled by the fact that the pathetic thing had been a gift from Aunt Emily. She had more than half a mind to go down, free the doll from its narrow prison, and make a plea for its presence at the party.

Lela would not be pleased. The large doll, with its small, stitched mouth and its ridiculous expression, was very poor at conversation and would constantly be dribbling tea down its dress. There would be a scene. Rather than risk that, Alice turned back to the book she had brought out with her.

It was Miss Witherspoon's history of hand puppets. She had taken several halfhearted runs at it before and been utterly unable to get past the first few pages. But today she had turned to the chapter devoted to the Punch-and-Judy play and found herself instantly captivated.

The birth and evolution of the play paralleled the rise of the working poor in the cities of the nineteenth century. Punch had long been a stock comic character in the marionette plays performed at local fairs; these plays generally appealed to the upper classes. It was only when Punch left the security of the fairgrounds for the uncertain life of the street as a hand puppet that he found his true audience.

As a street performer the Punchman was dependent for his living on the donations of the crowd he managed to attract. The plot had to be basic, the action lively, to induce the passerby to stop. To keep the action going and to avoid leaving the stage bare, it became convenient to keep Punch on stage and have the other characters pop in on him. As a hand puppet Punch was perfectly suited for action. He could move quickly and interact easily with the audience.

The crowds that stopped to see the play were mixed, but the poorest were the most appreciative. In Punch they saw a reflection of themselves. To them he was not an inhuman monster but a comical figure caught up in a chain of circumstances beyond his control. Far from being horrified by his deeds, in the spirit of the play they laughed, for they identified instinctively with Punch rather than his victims. As a puppet he was able to act out their own outrageous fantasies. In flouting authority he was a symbol of their own struggle for liberty.

Alice closed the book. She looked down at the black-and-white photo on the back of the dust jacket. It showed a young Miss Witherspoon at the basement workbench, busy in the creation of some puppet.

It was a peculiar picture, peculiar in that it was so unlike the dour portrait dominating the office wall. There she seemed so stern, so unbending, every bit as wooden as one of her puppets. Here, however, the camera had captured a different mood.

Most striking were the eyes; they were not the icy eyes of the woman on the wall, the forbidding eyes of the old woman Alice remembered behind the counter. These rather were warm and gentle, and lent an unaccustomed softness to the face. They were the eyes of a mother fussing fondly over her child. Was that what they were, then, those many puppets she had so passionately collected and cared for—her children? And through them a love hidden behind the cold professional pose was let loose. That was why she was such a wonder with these puppets, because to slip inside their small world was to bring something to birth that otherwise would not be.

Alice thought immediately of Mother, upstairs in her small prison, the child she carried straining its small prison as well, both of them easing ever so slowly toward birth. How narrow a way it was, ringed on all sides with danger. Was this what motherhood meant? If so, she wanted nothing whatever to do with it. Better to sit in the sandbox and sip sand tea with Lela and her dolls.

She glanced up from the book, her eyes automatically scanning the yard for Lela. The sandbox was empty, the dishes scattered in the dirt. The door of the shed was shut.

Instantly alarm bells began to sound inside her. She got up from the chair, set the book down with conscious calmness, and looked back over her shoulder toward the house. There was not a trace of Lela or the doll.

"Lela. Lela?" she called, trying to ease the panic that was already starting to rear its ugly head.

She walked down to the shed, searched behind it, opened the door and peered into its mildewed depths.

Lela, you gave me such a fright. Don't you ever, ever do that again.

But there was no one there to scold.

The world had narrowed to a knife point. There was only the empty yard, the shrilling in her ears, the panic pushing its way up into her chest now, forcing the air from her lungs.

Be calm, stay cool, she tried to tell herself as she ran back through the thundering yard, calling, craning down into the dank underside of the stoop, imagining a momentary glimmer of devilish eyes in the dark; her gaze returning time and again to the sandbox, as though Lela might materialize there just as suddenly as she had vanished.

"Lela." Her voice sounded strangely hollow, impossibly distant, as though someone else entirely were speaking. "Lela, you come out this instant, you hear me?" But panic took the words and plucked them like a taut string stretched inside her, so that they came out quavering like an old woman's and lingered like echoes in the air.

She burst into the kitchen, the screen door snapping shut on her heels. Aunt Emily sat at the table hulling strawberries. She glanced up, smiled; then the smile fell away and she set the knife down in the dish with a clatter.

"Alice, what's the matter?"

"Did Lela come in—just now—a minute ago?"

"Why no, I thought she was—"

But already Alice had swept past her into the living room—empty—and up the stairs, fighting to slow herself down, to keep her footsteps measured; trying to push the crazy panic down, so as not to alert Mother that something was terribly wrong.

She *walked*, walked evenly, down the hall. The door of their bedroom was closed. Yes—Lela was in there; she had decided to invite another doll to the party after all. She had slipped past them unseen and was in there now debating which one to bring.

Alice would be calm with her; she would try not to lash out with the anger coiled just below her fear. She would simply grasp her firmly by the shoulders, tell her never again to run off without telling her. And that would be the end of it.

Lela was not in the room. Her toys and belongings were everywhere, like footprints in a muddy field. But she was nowhere. It was as if the earth had opened under her and swallowed her whole.

Alice stood momentarily at the window, her fingers white upon the sill; she stared numbly down into the impossibly empty yard. The sandbox looked alarmingly like a grave site. The panic had swelled into her throat now. Horrors burst like shellfire upon her brain. Newspaper nightmares: child disappearances, abductions, naked bodies discarded in the bush—

The woods, oh my God, the woods, she thought, and with a sudden horrifying certainty she knew that she would find her there. The room whirled about her, time sped irretrievably past. She had to stop it, stall it, somehow bring it to a halt so she could think. This couldn't be happening; it was like some terrible nightmare she would awaken from at any moment—like coming home from the library that dreadful day to find Mother lying motionless on the couch.

Her legs felt like rubber, ready to buckle beneath her, as she made her way back down the stairs.

"Lela. Lela, where are you?" a small voice screamed inside her. She ran back through the kitchen and came out onto the porch, just in time to see Aunt Emily squeezing by the loose board in the fence and disappearing into the woods.

As she tore through the yard after her, Alice crashed into the carriage, overturning it; dolls tumbled startled onto the grass.

The rain had started; the first heavy drops were pitting the sand in the box. She could hear them drumming on the canopy of leaves overhead as she entered the woods. Apart from that there was no sound; only a deep, uneasy silence,

broken by her panting and the crackle of dead leaves underfoot. The upper branches had begun to sway in some desperate dance. What sun there had been was utterly absent now.
A twilight dimness lay over all; and in that dimness shadows
took shape.

"Lela!" she cried, "Lela!" But the words were caught up
in the vast confusion of terror, a confusion that had taken
the once familiar stand of trees and turned it into an enormous forest, ancient and frightening. The trees towered
twice as high as they had before, grew twice as thick, and the
space between them was tangled now with thickets and
thorns, utterly impassable in places. What paths there had
been had vanished utterly, buried beneath the thick layer of
leaf mold blanketing the floor, as though no one had walked
here before.

In no time at all she was completely lost. She no longer
knew where the woods began, where they ended, what had
become of the tired brown stream that trickled through
them. Every way she turned there were the woods, stretching
on endlessly, the ancient gnarled trees pressing in on all
sides, their blighted trunks twisted into grotesque human
shapes, as in Lela's book of fairy tales.

No sooner had the thought of Lela, bent over her book,
knifed through the terror that encased her, than she saw a
small figure lying in the undergrowth at her feet.

It was Asha the doll, her hat pulled back off her head,
her hair flecked with dead leaves, smiling vacantly as Alice
stared down into her open eye.

A sound broke the stillness, a strange, disconcerting
sound, like a muffled burst of applause or the snapping of
wings as a flock of birds took flight. She wheeled around—
and instantly had the feeling she was no longer in the woods
at all, but back in her bedroom staring at the wallpaper by

the bed, the repeating pattern of leaves and stalks, the birds perched upon the branches, their beady eyes agape.

But now the pattern was impossibly alive. She could see the wind lashing the leaves, hear the fitful rustling of wings as the birds shifted nervously about. Something moved behind the pattern now, some nightmare shape, quietly quivering the stalks, testing the space between, seeking escape. It came ever nearer, nearer, until suddenly she caught a glimpse of eyes glaring between the branches, a flash of smile that widened like a wound in the shadows.

She screamed. The scene shivered down like dead leaves in the wind. And suddenly she was watching Lela running through the trees toward her, with Aunt Emily walking along behind.

Alice scooped her sister up in her arms, pressed her to her breast, felt the flutter of that tiny heart against her own. She didn't say a word, she just stood clutching her like a priceless treasure, wishing that their separate bodies might fuse magically into one. She stood there for a long time, tears rolling down her cheeks, and then Aunt Emily came, took Lela by the hand, and quietly led them from the woods.

Amanda had been deposed from her privileged position in the cradle beside the bed and lay along with the other dolls beneath a flannel blanket on the floor by the window. For tonight at least, Asha had taken her place; she lay there quietly, in unaccustomed luxury, her head couched upon the small feather pillow, her broken eye half opened on the night while she struggled toward sleep.

Others struggled as well. When she came to bed herself, Alice had discovered Lela lying wide-eyed and still in the lower bunk when she leaned in to kiss her.

"Still not asleep?" she said. "It's late. Turn over on your tummy now and close your eyes, okay?"

Lela turned obligingly, and Alice tucked the sheet around her shoulders and kissed her on the cheek.

"Turn on the fan?" said the small voice in the dark.

"All right, but you go to sleep now."

It had nothing to do with the weather, her wanting the fan; the room was cool and the rain continued to patter lightly on the windowpane. It had rather to do with magic.

Last fall, when Lela was in the throes of a seemingly endless spate of nightmares that had her waking in the night for weeks on end, crying inconsolably, Mother had managed to quiet her with the fan, concocting the story that it would blow away the bad dreams. It was a way of getting her back to sleep. In short order it became the only way of getting her to sleep, period.

All winter long the fan had stationed itself on the dresser, flailing its metal arms, dutifully keeping the dreams at bay. When Alice moved back in with her, she was driven almost to distraction with the constant whir and click of the blades against the metal guard and frigid air being blown around the room.

It was spring before she had managed single-handedly to break Lela of the habit, preferring in the warm weather that almost immediately followed to swelter in the airless room rather than start it up again.

But now the rhythmic whir and click seemed almost comforting as she lay curled in the dark, purposely averting her eyes from the wallpaper by the bed, listening instead to the light wakeful breathing from the bunk below, the small fitful noises from the next room, the faint rustle of sheets as the dolls shifted in their sleep.

They had entered into a pact of silence, the three of them. Lela, for her part, had refused to offer any explanation for why she had wandered off. She had sat in the kitchen after they got back, clutching her doll, keeping a stony silence that teetered on the edge of tears.

"Don't tell Mom and Dad," she pleaded. "Please don't." And, of course, they hadn't.

Any questions Father might have had about the suspicious silence that seemed to flow among the three of them was instantly stilled by the onion-smothered steak Aunt Emily set before him. His mouth opened in amazement and he gave himself up to ecstasy.

Lela tossed fitfully on the lower bunk, muttering something in her sleep. Why had she wandered off like that? What had she been thinking of? Anything might have happened to her. As Alice lay in the dark, the full horror of her own confusion in the suddenly alien woods washed over her again, the sense of imminent menace that rose around her with the rich damp smell of leaf mold.

She shifted, and her eye fell on the wallpaper by the bed. Instantly she was standing in the woods again, staring as if in a nightmare at the impossible pattern of birds and stalks and branches. Again she heard the light flurry of applause, the rustling of wings as the birds fretted. Again she saw the faint quivering of the stalks as something patiently tested the space between, then the sudden glint of eyes among the leaves, and the nightmare grin.

Near dawn the rain finally stopped. In the front room Mother slept, Father spooned by her side, one limp arm draped in sleep over her swollen belly. Inside, the baby, wakeful now, bumped twice against the intruder on its world, to no avail. In the middle room, stretched out on the floor beside the empty crib, Aunt Emily dreamed yet again of a magic show she had seen as a girl. In the back bedroom Lela woke suddenly as though she had been shaken, sat up, rubbed her eyes, and peered warily about the shadowed room. She scrambled quietly from her bed, took Asha by the arm, and nimbly scaled the ladder to the upper bunk.

She crawled in beside Alice, closed her eyes, and was almost instantly asleep. Across the room the fan ticked and whirred its way toward dawn, keeping the dreams at bay.

Part Two

The sleeping and the dead
Are but as pictures; 'tis the eye of childhood
That fears a painted devil.

—Shakespeare, *Macbeth*

16

A PLASTIC STATUE OF THE VIRGIN
stood on the dashboard, hands folded in prayer, eyes
raised heavenward. She bobbed slightly on her rubber suction base each time the car hit a bump. The sun had
bleached most of the blue out of her robe, but had not
noticeably paled the blush on the roses at her feet or
dimmed the emerald sheen of the snake she was quietly
crushing underfoot. She was quite possibly praying for the
car. The car could use all the help it could get.

Dangling from the chrome post of the rearview mirror
above the Virgin's head was a cardboard pine tree deodorizer.
It was apparently there for show; there was not a trace of
pine in the potpourri of odors that claimed the interior of
the car—a combination of sunbaked books and stale cigarette butts. The ashtray under the dashboard was full to
overflowing.

Alice turned and looked out the passenger window, past
the chipped travel stickers, at the rush of hedgerows, fallen
fences, and endless fields of corn. A wood lot loomed up; a
sudden flash from that dreadful day in the woods the week
before superimposed itself on the scene. She felt the residue
of panic, still firmly lodged in her stomach, begin to edge
obligingly upward. She forced it down, coaxing herself wholly back inside the car, focusing her attention instead on the
dashboard Virgin and her rooted dance.

She had no idea where they were going—or why. When
she'd stumbled down to breakfast that morning, it had been
to find Aunt Emily sitting alone at the kitchen table,

cradling a cup of coffee, her Shakespeare open in front of her. It was exactly the way she had left her the night before when she went to bed. Lying across the open pages was a scrap of paper covered in scrawl. A familiar enough sight; she was always jotting things down, cramming bits of scribbled paper into her pockets. Her aunt closed the book on it as Alice came in.

"Have you been up all night?" asked Alice.

"So it seems." There were deep circles etched around her eyes.

"You must be exhausted."

"Yes, I must be." She got up, went over to the sink, and rinsed her cup. For a long while she stood as if in a trance, staring at the calendar taped to the side of the fridge.

"Alice," she said finally, "we have to talk."

"About what?" asked Alice.

"About everything," she said, turning to her. "Everything." There was something in the tone of her voice, in the strange fixed look that cut through the fatigue in her eyes, that froze Alice to the bone.

"I'm going to get some sleep," continued her aunt. "When I get up I'd like you to come for a drive in the car with me—and we'll talk."

She left the room. Alice listened to her footsteps on the stairs, heard her quietly close the door of the middle room behind her.

She stared down at the volume of Shakespeare on the table. In a matter of minutes Lela would be down, demanding to be fed. She sat down and quickly fanned through the book until it fell open on the scrap of paper. It marked the opening page of the play *Macbeth*. The first few lines of the play were underscored with pencil:

FIRST WITCH: When shall we three meet again?
In thunder, lightning, or in rain?
SECOND WITCH: When the hurlyburly's done,
When the battle's lost and won.
THIRD WITCH: That will be ere set of sun.
FIRST WITCH: Where the place?

This last line was repeated on the scrap of paper, repeated time and again in that fierce, hurried scrawl, forming a circular pattern on the page. And at the center of the circle, in bold block letters from which the question sprang like spokes, a date—August 8.

The car was a world unto itself. This, Alice suddenly understood, was her aunt's real home. It showed in the way she drove the car, in the way her hands cradled the wheel as if it were alive, in the ease with which she met the ribbon of road unwinding before her. Within these narrow confines she was secure, safe, suddenly assured. All traces of the timid creature living among them fell away.

Hers was a world in motion. For the first time, Alice realized how difficult it must have been for her aunt to make a place among them—to suddenly stand still. That was why she seemed forever poised for flight; it had become her natural state.

To have asked Alice to accompany her today had been to invite her into that most secret part of herself. This cocoon of glass and rust and moving metal, with its books and papers and cigarette butts, contained her like a second skin. Here she was complete. It was Alice now who was the intruder.

But why had she invited her? What was it that she had

115

to talk about? They had scarcely said a word since leaving the house over an hour ago. Weaving slowly through the city as if repeating a familiar ritual, they had first stopped on a quiet tree-lined street beside an old bungalow with a Sold sign staked in the wild grass out front. There was a hole beside it where another house had been. Soon, she sensed, there would be two holes.

"Do you know this house?" Aunt Emily had asked.

"No."

"No, I didn't think you would. Well, once, a long while back, our family lived here. Your mother was just a little girl at the time. I was about your age. You know, it's strange, but part of me is living there still. I guess it always will."

As they drove off, Alice glanced back at the empty building poised on the edge of the pit. Someday the house they lived in now would no doubt fall to the same fate. Would the memories of their life there fall with it?

They drove for a short while and stopped a second time before leaving the city, this time at the town house development near the site of the old train depot. A boy in leather, perched on the ravaged wall surrounding the project, watched them with predatory eyes as they sat at the curb in the car.

"You know, when I was your age, none of this was here," said Aunt Emily, half to herself. "I keep stopping here now, half expecting it to be suddenly swallowed up by the ravine that was here then. I keep expecting to see the old train station standing perched on the far side."

"I've only seen pictures of it," said Alice. "It had burned down before I was born."

"Yes. Yes, I know. It's still burning."

It was a strange, chilling thing to say, made stranger still by the feral look of the young man sitting on the wall. Alice felt the cold finger of fear on her neck.

The city now was far behind. As they drove along the two-lane blacktop somewhere outside of Caledon, Aunt Emily suddenly leaned forward and pushed in the cigarette lighter knob on the dashboard.

"Forgive me," she said as she reached into her bag and came out with the package of cigarettes Alice had seen pushed down the side of the box in her room that day. She shook one out. The lighter popped; she touched the glowing coil to the tip. The dashboard Madonna was briefly enshrouded in smoke. The countryside unfurled calmly before them.

Then, from out of nowhere, came the question.

"Did you find what you were looking for the other day—in my room?"

It was as if someone had punched her in the stomach.

"Did you?"

"Yes." Now was not the time for lies.

"And was it this?" Her aunt reached into the bag again. This time her hand came out clutching the knife.

"Yes."

The Virgin bobbed on her rubber base. The car hurtled through the void like a stone dropped down a dark well. Alice felt her back fuse to the seat.

"Have you said anything about it—anything at all—to anyone?"

Alice shook her head.

"Good." The knife disappeared back inside the bag. They drove on in silence. Alice could hear the blood pounding in her ears. The sound seemed to thunder through the car.

"What must you think of me, I wonder," said Aunt Emily finally. "I shudder to think. I so wanted to shield you from this. But now I can't, not after this, not after what happened with Lela." She took a long drag of the cigarette, then leaned forward on the steering wheel and started off down the road.

"Wouldn't it be wonderful just to ride and ride and ride, to leave everything far behind and end up someplace where there was nothing to fear, someplace where everyone was as sweet and innocent as little Lela and nothing could ever happen to hurt them?"

She rolled the window down a touch to clear the smoke. The sudden rush of air snatched at her hair, loose strands flamed out from her head. The smoke whirled about her face. She drew a deep breath.

"You're not going to believe a word of what I'm going to tell you," she said. "Nor should you, I suppose. No more than I did twenty-eight years ago when I was told. But nonetheless, it's true." She turned and looked Alice full in the face. "Every single word of it—I swear."

The interior of the car thrummed with unreality. It whistled with the wind through the narrow gap in the window, so that Alice had to strain to hear.

"I was about your age," Aunt Emily began. "No longer a child, not quite a woman yet—a stranger to both worlds. Not a comfortable age, as I'm sure you know. I knew perfectly well what I didn't believe in, but what exactly I did believe was a mystery to me.

"One thing I definitely did not believe in was magic. I had put that behind me with the fairy-tale books I used to read. I was far too old for such nonsense.

"And then that summer—we were living in the house I

showed you—I got a call from the woman who'd taught me that year: Miss Potts?"

"Irma Potts."

"That's right. The book you came looking for in my room had been hers as a child. She gave it to me. I used to read it to my brother Albert the way you read it to Lela. She gave me many things. I left most of them behind when I left Caledon; and yet I've left nothing behind. Strange. There is no end to the strangeness of things."

She took a final drag of the cigarette and butted it in the ashtray. The whistling of the wind was like a wail. She rolled the window up; the silence fell over them like a bell jar. Into that silence she spoke.

"Miss Potts contacted me that summer to ask me about a flier she had found in a desk at school. It was a flier for a magic show. I knew the flier she was talking about, but I had no idea where it had come from. It had simply appeared one day on my desk.

"Still, when I got together with her soon after, she took me into her confidence and told me an incredible story. It concerned a magic show she had attended in the waiting room of the Caledon depot when she was a girl, and a magician so malevolent that the mere memory of him terrified her still.

"She was convinced that a boy who had attended the show had died soon after as a direct result of having participated in it. The flier she had found in my desk was the flier for that very show.

"As the summer went on, we met from time to time. She grew increasingly distraught, convinced that somehow, in some way, that show was about to take place again. You see, she had discovered that the day on which the date of the original show fell, a Saturday, August 8, was the same day on which that date would fall again that summer. To her it was more than mere coincidence that the flier announcing the show had suddenly reappeared. She was convinced that something was poised to happen at the depot on that night.

"Of course, I thought she was crazy. More than fifty years had passed since she had seen that show. The magician himself was likely long dead. The depot had been boarded up, unused for years. How could anything possibly happen there?

"But it made me uneasy all the same. You see, my father was working at the depot that summer. It was to reopen in the fall as a railway museum, and he had volunteered to help with the renovations. When the eighth of August finally arrived, my father was late returning from the depot. I grew worried and decided to go down myself to see that he was all right.

"It was raining hard, I remember. When I arrived at the depot it was dark. There didn't seem to be any signs of life. Yet as I walked through that door, something happened. I don't have the words for it, even now. It was as if I stepped from one world into another. And the world I entered was that of the magic show.

"It was like entering a dream. There was a stage, there were children seated on the floor, and in the air an overwhelming odor of roses. But it is the magician, Professor Mephisto, I remember most. I close my eyes and I can see him now, that bloodless face, those piercing eyes. An overwhelming aura of evil emanated from him.

"His voice was like music, infinitely seductive. The children sat there spellbound, hanging on his every word. He could have asked them to do anything and they would have done it.

"The climax of the show was an illusion called the

Decollation of John the Baptist, in which an assistant to the magician was seemingly beheaded. At the show Miss Potts had attended, the boy who had assisted in that illusion had later died. She had come to believe that anyone who accepted the magician's invitation to come on stage and assist him was fated to die.

"He asked for a volunteer. A boy stood up, someone I recognized. I tried to stop him, and the magician turned his power on me. He urged me to come up instead. He spoke gently, like a parent to a troublesome child, but below the surface another voice, cold, bloodless, sounded inside me. There was nothing I could do to stop myself. He commanded me to come, and I came. He commanded me to lie down, and I lay down. He could make you see things that weren't there, think things that weren't happening.

"If Miss Potts had not arrived on the scene, I would certainly have died, perhaps not then, but certainly later, as all the others had, all those strange spellbound children in the audience. Instead, the magician was thwarted, the spell was shattered, and we were left alone in the empty depot.

"All that remains of that night is a crumbling playbill in a display case—and this knife. Yes, this is the knife he used in the show. It must have fallen through a gap in the floorboards that night and lain there until the fire turned it up.

"I made a promise to Miss Potts, a promise that I would be ready for him if he came back. For twenty-eight years a part of me has been waiting, watching, knowing that the night would come around again and that when it did I would have to be here. I am here now.

"This year, for the first time since that night, day and date align as they did then. I don't expect you to understand. I don't know whether I do myself. But something in me dreads the approach of that date, and will not rest until it is

past. Already I sense some evil is abroad again, steadily gaining strength. Perhaps my coming here has lured it into your
midst. Perhaps that is why Lela wandered off the other day."

"But that's just crazy."

"Is it? Listen, Alice, there was something in the woods
that day, a sound. It led me to Lela. I think she followed that
sound into the woods. I think you heard it, too."

Alice looked at her and felt her blood run cold.

"I've heard that sound once before, Alice. That summer,
shortly before it all happened. I was out walking my little
brother, your uncle Albert, one afternoon. I'd stopped near
the depot to change him and when I'd finished he ran off
into the grass, playing. I was packing the things away when I
heard it—a distant, hollow sound, like hands clapping or the
flapping of wings when a flock of birds lifts off. But there
were no birds.

"Albert heard it, too. It seemed to come from the direction of the depot, and he ran to see what it was. By the time
I got there, he had already disappeared inside. The door had
been left open. By then I was frightened. The place was
deserted. There was clutter everywhere: broken plaster, piles
of rubbish; in one spot the ceiling had come through. I
found him in the waiting room. He was standing at the foot
of a staircase, looking up into the dark. I was sure there was
someone, something up there. I took him and ran from the
place as if the devil himself were on my heels.

"I cannot think of the magician or of that terrible night
of the show without remembering the overpowering odor of
roses. It was like his calling card. When I found Albert in the
depot that day he was holding a rose petal in his hand.
When I found Lela in the woods she had this."

In the palm of her hand lay a withered rose.

Suddenly it was all too much: the car, the shuddering of

the statue, the overflowing ashtray. Alice felt as if she might be sick. She rolled down the window and took deep breaths of air, greedily, the way a newborn takes the breast. Gradually the dreadful sense of nightmare passed, and the nausea with it.

"Alice. I don't expect you to believe all this. It sounds utterly insane, I know. But please, be careful. Watch out for Lela. Keep away from the woods. If anything happened to either of you I could never forgive myself."

"And what will you do?"

"Watch, wait. I had thought that the depot would be the place. Now that it's gone, I don't know. Perhaps the site where it stood, that town house project. I just don't know."

Alice remembered the day she'd come home and discovered this strange woman telling Lela the story of the gingerbread boy being chased by the fox and coming across a big old car parked by the side of the road.

And that old car swung open its door and said, "Hop in, little gingerbread boy, we're heading the same way, you and I."

She glanced in the rearview mirror back down the stretch of dusty road they had just traveled. Was there something back there, just beyond the last rise in the road, slowly gaining on them?

17

Punch and Judy

V

Curtain opens on scene 2—a prison window is in view with PUNCH behind the bars, a view of the woods beyond.

Enter JACK KETCH. He fixes the gibbet on the platform of the stage, then exits.

PUNCH: Well, I say, that's very pretty. That must have been the gardener. And what a lovely tree he's planted just opposite the window, for a view.

Enter CONSTABLE. He places the ladder against the gibbet and exits.

PUNCH: Stop, thief! Now there's a rascal for you. He'll be back shortly to steal the fruit from that tree, I'll wager.

Enter JACK KETCH with coffin. He sets it down on the platform and exits.

PUNCH: What's that for, I wonder? Oh, I see now. It's a basket to put the fruit in.

Enter JACK KETCH.

KETCH: Now, Mr. Punch, you may come out, if you wish.

PUNCH: Thank you very kindly, but I'm quite happy here. This is a nice place—and such a lovely view.

KETCH: But you must come out. You are ordered to be executed.

PUNCH: What's that?

KETCH: You are to be hanged by the neck till you are dead—dead—dead.

PUNCH: Hanged? Oh dear, oh dear. And three times over?

KETCH: No, only once.

PUNCH: But you said dead—dead—dead.

KETCH: Yes, and when you are dead—dead—dead you will be quite dead. And now, prepare yourself for execution.

PUNCH: No—you could not be so cruel.

KETCH: Then why were you so cruel as to commit so many murders?

PUNCH: But that's no reason you should be cruel too, and murder me.

KETCH: Come along.

PUNCH: But I don't want to be hanged. I've got a sore throat already.

KETCH: Well, then, I must fetch you (*he goes into the prison; there is a struggle*).

PUNCH (*as* KETCH *drags him out to the front of the stage*): Mercy, mercy! I'll never do it again, I swear.

18

BY THE TIME ALICE WAS FINISHED making the third and final sign for the show, the fumes from the Magic Markers were definitely getting to her. She was feeling woozy and light-headed and more than a little sick to her stomach.

What she needed was air. She had tried earlier to coax open the workroom window, but along with most of the other windows in the old building, it had been painted shut years ago and would not budge.

Now she resorted to brute force. Rifling through the supply cupboard where she had discovered the markers, she found a large utility knife. She ran it repeatedly around the sash of the window, gouging a channel through the grimy paint, then tried opening the window again. This time, after a brief struggle, there came a loud cracking sound, like the breaking of bones, then a long, low groan as the paint gave way and the window grated open an inch or two. Fresh air streamed into the room, cutting through the cloying odor of the markers, blowing chips of paint to the floor. She capped the markers, shut them away, then stood back to admire her handiwork:

PARKVIEW PUBLIC LIBRARY PRESENTS
THE TRAGICAL COMEDY OF PUNCH AND JUDY
A PUPPET SHOW FOR YOUNG AND OLD
SATURDAY, AUGUST 1
—10:30—

In the upper right corner she had attempted to draw a picture of Punch, wielding his stick and grinning his crazy grin. The first two attempts were rather pathetic, but the third was not half bad. She had managed in that one to make him look both devilish and endearing. This, she was beginning to understand, was the secret of Punch's appeal.

In the upper left corner she had sketched the puppet theater itself, complete with stars and quarter moons. The curtain was closed. It had been easier to draw it that way, of course, but there was something else that lay behind her doing so—the growing wish that it really would stay closed.

Doing up the posters had really brought it home. The show was less than three weeks away. No longer a vague commitment hovering comfortably in the distance, it was clear and concrete now, and bearing down inexorably upon her. Already there were foreboding flutters in the pit of her stomach.

She rooted through the shelves until she found a roll of masking tape. With it and the posters in hand, she went to find Mr. Dwyer.

The library lay still and dark; only the scattered security lights still shone, casting long shadows, making the familiar suddenly strange and unsettling. Mr. Dwyer's office was dark, the door closed. She glanced anxiously up at the clock above the desk. It was after seven; she was already later than she said she'd be. Staying on late was getting to be a bad habit, a habit she intended to break.

From the Children's Room came the uncanny sound of voices. She came as far as the doorway—and stopped. There in the shadows stood the puppet theater, its stage suddenly ablaze with light. She had a fleeting image of children clustered eagerly around it in the dark.

Mr. Dwyer was acting out the scene in which Punch, now imprisoned, is confronted by the hangman, Jack Ketch. Stage left stood the gibbet. Beside it lay the small open coffin. Punch, in his innocence, thinks it is a basket for collecting the fruit of the tree.

The more she came to know of the play, the more strongly Alice's sympathies lay with Punch. She had grown increasingly uncomfortable with the idea of the Devil carrying him off in the end. It was this more than anything else that disturbed her about Jacob Hubbard's version of the play. According to Miss Witherspoon's book, in the early days of the play Punchmen were often pelted with mud by the crowd and driven away for daring to give the Devil the victory.

Punch in the end was not really wicked; he was simply impetuous. Like a child, he did not think things through. Throwing the baby out the window meant no more to him than Lela throwing the doll out of the sandbox in sheer frustration with it, or than her own foolish wish about the baby that night in bed. He did not deserve damnation.

Her own doubts were made all the more acute in light of the fact that Mr. Dwyer had so passionately thrown himself into the play. When she'd mentioned her unease with the ending to him, pointing out that in Miss Witherspoon's book she'd found an alternate text in which Punch in fact got the better of the Devil, he had been unimpressed. Of course there were other, perhaps even more common endings to the show, he'd said, but this was the text that went with this show—an early and very rare text, at that—and he was determined to follow it to the letter.

She found his passion for conformity, his utter inability to waver one iota from the script as it stood, infuriating. The more they progressed in preparing for the show, the more rigid and remote he became. It might simply have been the way he dealt with his own undoubted nervousness about it that made him seem suddenly so severe, but still it was hard to sympathize.

The show had become an obsession with him. It was all he talked about, all he appeared to think about. Yesterday he'd spent the better part of the afternoon shut away in his office laboring over a little balsa wood coffin for the show, oblivious of all else. He had dropped the running of the library squarely in her lap. It hardly seemed fair. Her initial enthusiasm for the project, for the job itself, had waned. Much of the quirkiness in his manner had returned as well; she found herself constantly watching his hands.

The scene came to a close with Jack Ketch dragging Punch screaming from his cell to the front of the stage. The puppets dropped from sight. There was a momentary silence, then Mr. Dwyer's muffled voice from behind the stage.

"Well, how was that?"

"Good, very good." And it was. In fact, it was hard to see why he needed her at all. He had practically the whole script down by heart himself.

"The voices carry all right?"

"Yes, just fine."

He popped out from behind the stage, stripping off the black sleeves that covered his bare arms.

"Boy, that's hard work alone—doing both voices, keeping both hands up and moving for that length of time. I'm glad you'll be there to do Punch. These old wooden puppets are heavy, not like the papier-mâché things we use now. Old Jacob Hubbard must have had incredible strength to do a whole show alone, and not just once, mind you, but as much as a dozen times a day. Incredible. Ah, I see you've finished the posters. Let's have a look."

She held them up while he took a couple of steps back and made a show of admiring them.

"Excellent. Now, let's see, where do you think we should hang them?"

It was decided that they should tack one to the bulletin board in the adult section, tape another to the pillar at the entrance to the Children's Room, and hang the third on the wall behind the main desk. They roamed the shadowy building putting them in place.

"Do you think you might have time to do a quick run-through of one of the scenes before you go? I was thinking—"

"Sorry, I can't tonight. I promised I'd be home."

"It wouldn't take long. I could give you a lift afterward." She watched as he stretched across the counter to reach the day calendar attached to the pillar, watched his hand spring and snatch away the sheet bearing today's date, crumpling it into a ball, then snatch away the next as well. Now a bold black 13 showed—Monday's date.

"No, really, I can't." She was utterly determined not to be coaxed into staying again.

A familiar pained expression stole over his face as his hands toyed with the crumpled paper. It was as if she'd just wounded him—deeply, willfully. She kept down the guilt it strove to summon up and headed firmly for the door.

"I'll see you Monday," she said as she turned the lock. He stood silently in the doorway to the Children's Room, the poster taped to the pillar beside him. The shadows, along with the lighted theater behind him, made of his figure a dark, featureless silhouette.

"Have a nice weekend," she called over her shoulder as

she was leaving, but he had already turned and begun to walk back to the theater. At the spot where he'd been standing, the crumpled paper lay upon the floor.

She was glad for the fresh air. Her stomach still felt queasy from the marker fumes; the muscles in her neck were stiff with tension. She walked quickly down the lurching flagstone walk and out the gate, not bothering to look back at the building, anxious to put some much-needed space between herself and it. She felt relieved that tomorrow was Sunday.

She wished with all her heart that she'd never taken that drive with her aunt last weekend, wished that she'd never been told the incredible story of that magic show, had never been burdened with her aunt's belief that it would somehow return. She could not put it out of her mind. It was creating ripples of unease everywhere.

Before then, she had been more than willing to work late with Mr. Dwyer on the project, more than ready to shrug off the intensity of his interest in it as simple enthusiasm. Now, the mere thought of the two of them alone, with the old building cast in shadow around them, suddenly terrified her. She thought of the crumbling playbill lying in the display case on the floor above them, the empty space on the felt where the knife had been, and she wanted to run.

Most frustrating of all was the fact that she could share the story with no one. It was this terrible sense of being near to bursting with the need to tell someone what she was feeling that was driving her crazy.

She yearned to reach back and recover that sense of kinship she'd felt for Mr. Dwyer at the beginning, to simply sit down and unburden herself to him. But even if she could somehow pierce his preoccupation with the play, to do so would be to betray her aunt. And so she was left with the unease, an unease which only grew and festered with being shut away.

Wasn't that in the end the cause of it all: the fact that Aunt Emily had shut her feelings inside for so long that they had mutated finally into this madness? There was no doubt that something had happened to her that August night long ago, but time had twisted it into something so incredible that it had swallowed reality completely.

But what of that sound in the woods that day? She too had heard that. The library lay behind her now, yet Alice still was ill at ease. She kept glancing back over her shoulder, imagining faint, scurrying footsteps following her. The street, which would normally have seemed welcoming enough, wore a somehow sinister face now. Where she would ordinarily have seen light and life, she sensed a creeping decay.

The old shops that lined the narrow street wore fissured, garishly painted faces: a fruit store, rank garbage piled before its darkened windows; a bakery, closed for the night, cakes and pastries left in the window, a large fly feeding on a cherry tart; a butcher shop, still open, the familiar smell of sawdust and blood wafting through the open door, a small, shriveled woman watching the butcher weigh a bloody piece of something on a scale. Images of Father's shop, the huge freezer hung with waxen sides of beef, entered her mind. She saw the clock on the wall behind the counter and quickened her pace. Seven-thirty. Father would be home now, sitting in the chair with a beer, reading the weekend comics with Lela curled up on his lap.

Lela. How incredibly vulnerable she suddenly seemed since the day in the woods. How incredibly vulnerable they all seemed, their little lives like fragile candle flames. The house had once seemed so secure, an impregnable fortress, immune to attack. Now a ragged crack ran through the wall from top to bottom and a chill wind blew among them. She felt herself running desperately from one to the next, cupping her hands around the flickering flames.

Something had opened that crack, had let the darkness whistle in, as the wind had whistled through the car window while Aunt Emily told her incredible tale. Could such things possibly be? No, the voice of reason screamed inside her. But another part of her—the part that sank beneath the spell of the *Wonder Book* as readily as Lela, that looked in the window of the little cottage and saw the withered face of the witch take shape among the shadows, the part that had lain in bed that night and wished the dreadful wish that the baby were never born—that part heard the light fall of footsteps behind her now and turned yet again to stare nervously down the empty street.

19

SINCE THE TV DIED, FATHER HAD been faithfully laboring his way through *Six Practical Lessons for an Easier Childbirth*. He had, of course, become an expert on the subject.

Each night after dinner he would plant himself solemnly in his chair, read slowly through the next section, then disappear upstairs with Mother to practice relaxation exercises and breathing techniques behind closed doors. No one was allowed in, but Lela had taken to creeping quietly up the stairs to eavesdrop on the intriguing sounds of panting, blowing, and shallow breathing coming from the room.

Tonight, with dinner done and the dishes stacked by the sink, they were ready for their first public demonstration. The family gathered in the living room. Mother lay down on the floor, a pillow at her head, another under her knees. She looked a little like a beached whale. Father knelt down by her side.

"All right. I want you to take a deep cleansing breath, then relax your whole body." He checked her relaxation by lifting an arm, a leg, then letting it fall limply to the floor.

When he was satisfied that Mother was completely relaxed, he explained to the audience sitting on the couch that they were going to simulate a contraction. Clamping a hand on her thigh, he studied the sweep hand on his watch. The idea was that by relaxing the body and breathing along with the contraction, one could help control the pain of labor and delivery.

"Okay, the contraction's beginning." Mother took a deep cleansing breath, then began to breathe slowly, rhythmically.

"Remember, shallow breaths. Focus on a spot on the ceiling. Okay, fifteen seconds; the contraction's getting stronger." The pressure of his hand on her leg intensified. "Stronger still." Mother breathed more rapidly now, short panting breaths. Lela sat wide-eyed on Aunt Emily's knee, taking it all in.

"Forty-five seconds," announced Father. "The contraction's going now. Going." He eased up the pressure on her thigh. Mother's breathing slowed. "Okay, the contraction is over. Take a deep cleansing breath."

"There," he said. "Nothing to it."

"Is the baby coming now?" asked Lela, looking for tell-tale legs hanging below the hem of Mother's maternity top.

"No, dear, not yet," said Mother as Father helped her to her feet. "But soon now—very soon."

Aunt Emily brought in tea and fresh gingerbread she had baked. Nobody baked gingerbread like Emily. They sat for a while and talked while it disappeared from the plate. For a sacred moment their lives were one, encased in an impregnable shell of security. Alice luxuriated in it while it lasted.

It was Aunt Emily who broke the spell. She excused herself, gathered up the cups and plates, then pulled on her old cloth coat and quietly left the house. It had reached the point of ritual now, these after-dinner walks. It would be well past dark before she returned, and more likely than not she would head straight upstairs to her room.

Where she went remained a mystery. For Father it was a matter of growing concern. He did not like the idea of her wandering the streets in the dark. Caledon had changed since she was a child, he told her. One had to be careful; some neighborhoods were no longer considered safe.

She would patiently listen while he lectured her, but the routine remained unchanged.

It had begun to drizzle shortly after she'd left the house, but Emily did not dare turn back for an umbrella. She walked quickly down the rain-spattered street. Night would come early; she must hurry. The onset of darkness caused her growing unease.

She let her feet lead her now, refusing steadfastly to think about where they would lead. She could have taken the car, but taking the car did not work. She felt far too secure in the car, far too safe. She would only end up driving in maddening circles around the circumference of terror, utterly unable to coax the wheels inward, reduced at last to sitting parked in the dark somewhere, smoking endless cigarettes.

No, walking was the only way: no escape, no ready refuge, nothing to do but carry through with it, convinced that her very vulnerability would lure the thing she sought into showing itself.

She crossed under the train bridge. A figure hunched in the shadows, clutching a paper bag, peered at her as she passed. Only an old man, waiting out the rain. She hurried uphill toward the corner, passing the driveway to the poultry plant. Brought them in by the truckload, stacked in cages, two to a cage. Criminal. Fresh Daily, read the sign. Hanging by the necks against the wall in rows, heads shrouded in butcher paper, featherless. The rain woke the smell of blood in the alley. The gutter ran red. She hurried on, turned the corner at the lights, glancing in the window of the storefront palm card reader. Your future foretold. Man with a goiter sitting in a wheelchair watching TV.

As she neared the library she glanced up. Her eyes scanned the lancet windows, settling on the one beneath which she knew the damaged display case stood. A shiver ran through her, as again she felt the glass slice her hand like a razor.

She looked down, saw a light burning in the basement, illuminating the bushes hugging the building. For reasons she could not explain, the light troubled her. It made the structure seem somehow alive, as though that light were its secret heart, beating steadfastly against the stone, threatening to wake it into flesh.

The rain had begun to pick up. Puddles pooled on the pavement; cars hissed past. She was afraid, so desperately afraid. Less than two weeks remained now. Time had slipped through her hands like sand. Twenty-eight years. Twenty-eight years reduced in an instant to this. She was no more prepared now than she had been then. Somehow the darkness would surprise her again. It would lunge when she least expected it, from a direction she had not even imagined.

She was not equal to the task, could never hope to be. Why, in heaven's name, had it been laid upon her? Her every instinct told her to flee, to quit this place now before it was too late, to simply climb into her car and go. Yet if she did she knew she would never stop. Never. She would just drive on and on and on, until one day the earth opened under her and dirt began to rain down on the roof.

She must stop. She had stopped—here, now. This was the time; this, the place. She felt as if she had entered a dream. But it was not a dream. The danger was that she would begin to believe it was, that she would begin to doubt. Doubt would leave her utterly defenseless.

She turned up her collar, kept close to the storefronts to ward off the rain, pretended to peer into windows as she hugged her purse close, but saw in every one the same haunted face reflected back.

"Lord, let this cup pass from me," she caught herself muttering as she stood like a drowned rat on a street corner, waiting for the light to change. A little boy, sitting in a stroller eating ice cream, stared up at her. He reminded her achingly of Albert. A painted wooden doll dangled by a string from the frame. She smiled, then watched the child whisked away as the light turned and his mother hurried him across the street.

The wheels left evanescent tracks on the wet pavement. She followed in their wake, sensing with chill intuition where they would lead. She had to stop herself from breaking into a run, from tearing up to the poor woman like some mad thing and pleading with her to turn back, turn anywhere but where she was headed. Instead, she kept her head down, clutched her bag close, and followed in the traces of their tracks.

When she glanced up again they were gone. And there directly before her lay the town house project. The stroller tracks veered off the sidewalk and disappeared down a path through the wall, like the end of a string threading into the labyrinth beyond.

She stood there paralyzed by the prospect of the place. Again that feeling washed over her, the sense that all this brick and glass were but the brittle carapace of some living thing swelling beneath, a thing which might at any moment shatter the shell and show itself.

How many times had she come here now? Each time forcing herself to follow the maze of winding paths that snaked through the project, looking covertly through curtained windows, staring at the same blank purple door repeated endlessly, sensing all the while how utterly vulnerable she was.

Some of the small fenced yards in front of the houses still bore the remnants of lawn, but most had lapsed into plots of barren soil tufted with weeds. There was rubbish everywhere: islands of it mounded at curbside for collection, more simply abandoned to the yards. Broken pieces of furniture, rusting shopping carts, gutted appliances. The place was still a dumping ground, as the ravine had been before. But now there were no trees to mask the decay; only these shabby, somehow desperate houses huddled against the dark.

Somewhere here, among all these ordinary dwellings, stood one extraordinary one. But where? What clue would it give to betray its presence? Something, something slightly amiss. But what?

Much as she dreaded the onset of darkness, the waking of lights in the houses helped her task. For the house she sought would not be full of life. It would not send out the comforting odors of cooking, would not light lamps against the night. No, the house she was searching for would be one with the night, would bear its stamp. It would be lying in wait, apparently still. Yet inside it something would be stirring, pacing the empty rooms relentlessly, like a wolf awaiting prey.

As she stood there now the old terror washed over her with renewed strength: the terror that she would wander into the bewildering maze and never find her way out again, that she would blunder unaware into the waiting arms of the beast.

The leaden sky lowered like a lid, and the darkness rose like mist to meet it. She clutched her bag close to her, felt the chill sleep of steel within, and let the fading tracks lead her in.

20

PUNCH AND JUDY

VI

PUNCH (*trembling, wringing his hands*): Oh dear, oh dear.

KETCH: Come along, Mr. Punch. Justice can't wait.

PUNCH: Wait a minute. I haven't made my will.

KETCH (*thinking*): Well, I suppose we can't let a man die until he's made his will.

PUNCH: You can't?

KETCH: Certainly not.

PUNCH: Then I don't think I'll make one at all (*attempts to exit*).

KETCH: Not so fast, Mr. Punch. Come along, put your head in this noose.

PUNCH: What's the news?

KETCH: This here is the noose.

PUNCH: Is it good news or bad news?

KETCH: Bad news for you, good for the public. Now, put your head in there.

PUNCH (*putting his head under the noose*): There?

KETCH: No, higher up.

PUNCH (*putting his head over the noose*): There?

KETCH: No, lower down—in there (PUNCH *falls down and pretends to be dead*). Get up, you're not dead.

PUNCH: Oh yes, I am.

KETCH: Oh no, you're not (*hauls him up*).

PUNCH: Please, sir, I've never been hanged before and I don't know how to do it.

KETCH: Very well, then, I'll show you. Watch me. First you put your head in the noose—like this, you see (*puts his head in;* PUNCH *watches attentively*)? Now, you see my head?

PUNCH: Yes.

KETCH: Well, when I've got your head in like this, I pull the end of the rope.

PUNCH (*pulling the rope a little*): Like this?

KETCH: Yes, only tighter.

PUNCH (*pulling a little more*): Like this?

KETCH: Tighter than that.

PUNCH: Good, I think I understand now.

KETCH: Splendid. Now, I'll take my head out and you put yours in. And when it's in you must turn to the ladies and gentlemen and say, "Good-bye, fare-you-well."

PUNCH (*pulls the rope quickly*): Good-bye, fare-you-well (JACK KETCH *is hanged*). Cock-a-doodle-doo. Look, here's a man tumbled into a ditch and hung himself up to dry.

21

THE FOLLOWING DAY ALICE DECIDED to take the shortcut home through the woods. It was the first time since the incident with Lela that she'd dared to set foot near them. But time had already dulled the horror of that day. She was tired, it was late, and the bag she was carrying was heavy on her back. The prospect of taking the long way home seemed suddenly childish.

She hurried along the flagstone walk that wound past the reflecting pool behind the library. There was actually water in the pool now. Last night's rain had made a soup of the dirt and dead leaves that lined the bottom of it.

She followed the path as far as the fence that bounded the library property. Past this point any pretense at civilization immediately disappeared. The grass, short and scorched on this side, instantly sprang wild. The path was swallowed up by earth and the all-encroaching grass, resurfacing now and then through the field as though desperately seeking air.

Despite her resolution, Alice had stayed for more than an hour after closing again today, putting the finishing touches on the puppet theater, brushing gold to the stars and quarter moons that graced the boards, red to the delicate scrollwork that framed the stage itself. Mr. Dwyer, meanwhile, fussed with the new curtain he'd fashioned from a piece of rich blue velvet flecked with stars. He'd found it in a remnant bin at the fabric shop while buying a length of black muslin for the backdrop.

Finally finished, they stood back to admire their handiwork. It was really quite striking, the delicate blue of the boards deepened by the twilight tones of the curtain, the gold and red highlights around the stage rich and wonderfully alive.

Alive, yes, he'd said so himself as he stood there by her side.

"It's as if we've brought it back to life."

A section of the chain link mesh had been peeled back like a flap of skin. As she squeezed through, her bag snagged on a sharp end of wire. The straps bit into her shoulder as she pulled free.

She started down the narrow trail of trampled grass that formed the path through the field. The electrical tower loomed before her like some monstrous, skeletal scarecrow. A chill ran through her.

The ground underfoot was soft, spongy with moisture. The grass groped at her legs with wet fingers as she pushed through it. She had the uneasy sensation that something lay lurking in it. Here and there the old flagstone path broke the surface and the grass yielded briefly before it.

She ran from island to island of stone until she reached the rise of the roadbed. The train tracks ran like a rusty seam through the field, binding the weeds and wild grass to the woods beyond. She stood on the weathered ties, perched momentarily between worlds, glad to be free of the field, uneasy at the prospect of entering the woods.

On the fringe of the woods she stopped and slid the pack from her shoulders. Along with half a dozen fairy tales she'd rooted out for Lela while she was shelving, the pack was weighted with two parcels carefully swathed in tissue paper.

With only a week left until the big performance, Alice

could already feel the panic taking her stomach in its smooth steel grip. Tonight, Mr. Dwyer had suggested that it might be helpful to her if she were to take Punch home for the weekend to practice the final scene in front of a mirror as Miss Witherspoon recommended in her book. While in the basement, wrapping the puppet carefully for the trip, he had offered as an afterthought to loan her the Devil puppet as well, so that she could run through both parts in the scene. It was, she realized, a vote of confidence in her, his way of trying to bridge the rift that had widened between them.

She opened the pack now and readjusted the books so that the sharp angles of the puppet heads would not press into her back. Nestled in the bottom of the bag in their tissue shrouds, they looked like the chrysalides of some strange creature undergoing metamorphosis.

As she buckled the bag closed again she glanced back at the library. There it sat, dark and silent, its great glass eye staring up into the sky. Seen from this distance, in the forgiving glow of twilight, the decay that quietly ate away at the building was all but invisible. For a moment the backdrop of office buildings downtown seemed to fall away, and it stood there solitary and proud, as timeless as the woods at her back.

She remembered the photograph that hung in Miss Witherspoon's room: the building surrounded by lush gardens, gently winding paths leading off into the woods, graceful figures strolling toward the waiting shadows.

Now as she picked her way along the narrow path among the trees, she imagined herself one of those shadowy ladies of the past, her long skirts rustling about her legs, the whalebone stays pinching her waist, her parasol resting on her shoulder. The path appeared to widen obligingly before her; here and there a patch of the original brickwork rose to meet her through the leaf mold. She let it lead her down to the small wrought-iron bench by the stream.

It was all but hidden in the undergrowth now, the rusted chain that shackled it to a tree biting deeply into the bark, the ghosts of lovers' names carved in the smooth gray trunk. She stood for a moment at the base of the tree, straining to make them out, unaware now of the weight of the pack on her back, caught up in the strangeness of time's passing.

A rustle in the undergrowth brought her back. The illusion shattered, leaving her alone in the darkening woods. She whirled around, startled.

"Who's there?" she called. Only the whisper of wind in the trees.

"Who is it?" And as if in reply a squirrel darted from the undergrowth and skittered up a tree. From the safety of a high branch it chattered angrily down at her.

A squirrel. She had probably frightened the poor thing half to death with her shouting. She laughed over the crazy thudding of her heart, scolding herself for being so foolish as to let her imagination get the better of her. There was nothing here to be afraid of, just as there had been nothing before. No sound of clapping, no beating wings, only the echo of her own panic turning the woods to terror.

Making her way down to the muddy bank of the stream, she leaped to the stone planted midway in the rusty water, and came safely to the other side. As she picked her way through the trees, working her way steadily toward home, she pretended to be perfectly calm. Still, the short trek seemed to stretch on forever, and by the time she came in sight of the shed and the high wooden fence, she found herself bathed in sweat.

Aunt Emily had nailed the loose board back in place. She would have to scale the fence. She slowed down to a deliberate shuffle, kicking up the leaf mold as she went. She was suddenly aware of a dull stabbing pain in her back. Feeling through the canvas of the backpack, she found that one of the puppets had shifted somehow and worked its way around the barrier of books she had set between herself and them. Even through the thick cloth of the bag and the tissue paper wrapping within, she could tell instantly which it was.

Father glanced up at the clock as she came through the kitchen door. They had delayed dinner for her again. Aunt Emily looked up from setting the table. She had made a soup; the house was heavy with the smell of it.

As she went to wash up, Alice brought a bowlful up to Mother on a tray. Over the past few days she had had some pains. The doctor had been by and suggested that from this point on, to be on the safe side, she spend most of her time in bed. She had been frightened into obedience.

Alice dropped her book bag in her room, washed quickly, and ran a brush through her hair. She yanked up her shirt and studied the angry red circle at the small of her back in the bathroom mirror. Tomorrow there would be a bruise.

As she came in with the tray she found Mother sitting on the edge of the bed in her housecoat, her feet dangling above the floor. She was massaging her bare belly with her fingertips in a light circular motion.

"Effleurage," she explained. "According to our resident expert it helps relax the muscles. The mystery guest seems to like it anyway. He's been kicking up a storm here. Look." She pointed to her stomach. There was a slight fleeting protrusion of the taut skin as a phantom limb poked outward from within, then vanished. For the first time Alice had the overwhelming sense of there being three of them in the room.

"I think it's a foot," said Mother. "Feels like a foot anyway. The doctor says the baby's head is down now. It won't be much longer, two or three weeks at most." She pulled her nightgown down and leaned over to look at the soup—cauliflower and broccoli florets floating in a vegetable broth.

"Mmm, delicious," she said, settling back in the bed, resting the bowl on the built-in bed tray of her belly as she began to eat.

Lela was of another opinion. She wanted nothing whatever to do with those "tree things," as she called them, floating on the top of her soup. She fished them out one by one and laid them on the plate where her bread had been. By the time she was finished there was nothing left in the bowl but a watery pink liquid with a few pathetic bits of tomato bobbing around in it. She pushed it away.

"I want another dinner," she announced.

Father tried to coax her into trying at least a little bit, but his heart just wasn't in it. Alice knew that if the four-year-old in him had its way he would have fished those little tree things out of his soup too. Even bribery, in the guise of a vanilla pudding with bananas on the bottom, failed to move her. At last she was faced with the choice of either eating "the delicious dinner" Aunt Emily had made for her, or going to bed hungry.

She mulled it over for something less than a second, then ran from the room. The next sounds they heard were her stamping off up the stairs and slamming the bedroom door shut behind her.

Aunt Emily remained silent through it all, staring steadfastly down at her plate. She had always been quiet, but her silence now exuded an almost palpable tension. Even Father felt it. Conversation quickly flagged, and the remainder of the meal was given over to silence, punctuated by periodic thuds overhead as Lela took out her fury on the dolls.

Father fled the scene as soon as possible, leaving Alice to toy with her banana pudding while Aunt Emily filled the sink and started doing the dishes.

To be alone with her aunt was exhausting. Just below the quiet surface, Alice sensed the rising anxiety in her as August drew near. She felt that she should say something. Yet what was there to say? The door that had opened briefly between them had closed and she dared not risk opening it again. She could not let herself be swept up in the foreboding. She *would* not let herself be swept up in it.

That, in the end, had been her reason for daring the woods today, to somehow shatter the spell she felt settling over them. And Aunt Emily knew it, too. The look she'd fixed Alice with as she walked through the back door had said quite clearly that she understood it all.

A somehow uneasy quiet had settled in above them. Finally Aunt Emily asked her to go up and peek in on Lela and see if she wanted to come down and have a bowl of cereal before she went to bed. Alice was more than glad to go.

She walked slowly up the stairs. From the front bedroom came the comforting sounds of Father's coaching and Mother's breathing as they ran through the evening ritual. The door to the middle room was closed. Alice recalled the haunted look in her aunt's eyes when she'd come in from her walk last night, the restless pacing that had lasted far into the night.

She walked quickly to the end of the hall now and opened her bedroom door. The first thing she saw were the dolls, lying dazed on the floor, their tea table overturned, the dishes scattered like shrapnel on the rug. Only then did she see Lela. She sat cowering in the shadows of the lower bunk, Asha clutched in her arms, staring fixedly at the far side of the room.

22

ALICE CAME SLOWLY INTO THE room and closed the door. She glanced over at her desk. Her book bag was open, the picture books strewn on the floor. Beside them, on a bed of crumpled tissue paper, lay the Devil, grinning his awful grin. Punch, still half-shrouded in paper, lay facedown on the floor nearby, his hump in the air.

She would have scolded Lela for going through her things had it not been for the look of utter terror in her sister's eyes.

"I don't like it," she said in a flat monotone, her eyes riveted on the puppet. "It's bad. It scared Asha. She's going to cry if you don't take it away from here. They're all going to cry."

It was clear that Lela herself was on the verge of tears. Alice crossed the room and picked the puppet up. "I've told you before not to touch my stuff, Lela. If you hadn't gone in my bag you would never have seen it."

"It's bad," said Lela again. "Bad. It has scary eyes, and it says things."

"Don't be silly, Lela. It's just a puppet." She slid her hand into the limp body, fed her fingers into the hollow head and the empty cloth arms. "See? Somebody made it out of wood. It can't hurt you." She took a step toward the bed.

Lela let out a piercing scream and buried her head in the blankets. Down the hall, Father called out, wondering what was the matter. Alice opened her bedroom door and assured him that everything was all right. Her eyes fell on Aunt Emily; the scream had brought her running. She was standing halfway up the stairs, her coat over her arm. Their eyes met briefly, then her aunt turned and started back down the stairs. In a few moments the front door closed with a quiet click behind her as she left the house.

Lela refused to come out of the blankets until the puppet was put away. Even then, all the while she was tidying the room before she went down for her bowl of cereal, she kept a wary eye on the book bag slung over the back of the chair.

She did not want one of the stories from the *Wonder Book* before bed that night. She settled on one of the new picture books Alice had brought home, fanning through it first to make sure no monsters lurked in its glossy pages.

Later, when Alice came to bed herself, she discovered the book bag lying in the bathtub. Lela had switched the fan on in the room. Like a fretful little bird, she had gathered up her entire brood of dolls and taken them into bed with her. Some, though still, remained awake, their wide button eyes gleaming dully in the dark. Wedged in among them, fast asleep, Lela seemed no more than a doll herself, a doll dreaming it was a little girl.

Waking in the morning to find the book bag back in the room, Lela quickly made herself scarce. For the rest of the morning she played downstairs, stationing herself in front of the broken television set, switching it on and off and on again, hoping against hope that the morning cartoons would magically appear. When they did not, she contented herself with drawing pictures on pieces of butcher paper cut from the huge roll Father had brought home from the shop, and taping them to the screen as substitutes. Aunt Emily sat quietly reading nearby.

Mother had passed a restless night and was sleeping now in her room. Father had reluctantly left her and gone into work for a few hours.

Alice, glad to have the bedroom to herself, spent the morning trying to commit the climax of the play to memory. The dolls had settled to their daily routine: some sat to tea at the table, others lounged in the sun against the wall by the window. She paced among them, script in hand, reading blocks of dialogue aloud, trying to imprint the pattern of words on her mind. It was a slow, laborious process, made doubly difficult by the fact that, despite Mr. Dwyer's explanations, she was still uncomfortable with the concluding scene of the play.

The puppets, unshrouded now, lay on the desk. There was a small chip on the Devil's forehead, newly inflicted by the look of it, likely the result of Lela's having dropped it in fright last night when she first looked into its leering face. Mr. Dwyer would no doubt notice it; she would not even be surprised to find him with a bandage on his own forehead the next time she saw him, as if in concert with the wounding of the puppet.

Lord, it was an ugly thing; there was no denying that. It lay there with its cadaverous face cracked and rayed with age, looking for all the world like an artifact unearthed from an ancient tomb. It had a primitive, somehow imperishable quality about it. If there was anything unnerving about it, it was this: that it seemed possessed of some dark, almost elemental life that had survived the centuries, smiling its unwavering wicked smile while people grew and withered around it. It was smiling still.

After lunch, Alice went down to the basement to unearth the old mirror that had once been mounted on the inside of the door of the downstairs closet. There was a warp in the glass that curiously distorted the image at a certain point midway along its length. Father had finally grown tired of its tricks and taken it down. It sat dejected now, furred with dust, quietly reflecting the underside of the stairs.

Aunt Emily had brought Mother up some lunch and then taken Lela to the park. Odd, thought Alice as she descended the scooped wooden stairs, the way Aunt Emily never comes down here. As if she were afraid. A regular nest of nightmares, that one. She took out the mirror, wiped it down, and carried it carefully up the stairs. The living room floor was awash with scraps of pink paper. One piece was still taped to the TV—stick figures armed with swords chasing off a horned monster. Upstairs, Mother played the radio in her room.

With some experimentation Alice found that if she wedged the mirror on its side between the mattress and the frame of the upper bunk, it was at a perfect level for practicing. She taped the script to the back of her desk chair and stationed the chair in front of her, then slid the puppets onto her hands—Punch on the right, the Devil on the left. She held them in front of her and slightly aloft, so that they appeared in the mirror.

Over the course of the next hour, she ran repeatedly through the scene, straining to keep the dialogue straight, coordinating the movement of the puppets with the action, trying to keep in mind the advice on puppet manipulation that Miss Witherspoon had given in her book: "The moment the puppet is slipped on the hand, it becomes one with you, endowed with life and spirit. Your hand is its body. It only permits you to move it."

It was exhausting work. In very little time her arms ached from the strain of holding the heavy puppets up. At first she was painfully aware of her face in the mirror, intruding on the scene, mouthing lines that the puppets themselves were to speak, reducing them to empty wooden shells on either side of her. But by degrees she learned to station her face in front of the warp in the mirror so that it was twisted first into something foreign, and finally into invisibility.

At that point the puppets came to life. The ache in her arms, indeed her arms themselves, seemed to vanish, and for a time out of time she became no more than an eavesdropper on the drama as it unfolded:

Enter PUNCH *with a stick. He dances about, beating time on the stage and singing.*
   PUNCH:

> *Foll de roll, foll de roll*
> *I'm the boy to beat them all.*
> *And here's a stick to thump Old Nick,*
> *If he by chance upon me call.*

Enter the DEVIL. *He peeps in at the corner of the stage, and exits.*
   PUNCH (*much frightened, retreating as far as he can*): Oh dear! O Lord! Speak of the devil, they say, and there he'll be. Who's there?

Dead silence while PUNCH *continues to stare steadily at the spot where the* DEVIL *appeared. The* DEVIL *peeps his head in at the opposite side of the stage.*
   PUNCH (*in a squeaking whisper*): Who goes there, I say? Is it the butcher?
   DEVIL: No, Mr. Punch.
   PUNCH: Who is it, then?
   DEVIL: It is I (*disappears again from view as* PUNCH *whirls in the direction of the voice*).

PUNCH (*terrified now, turning from side to side*):
And who is "I"? What do you want? Show yourself, I
say.

Enter the DEVIL.

DEVIL (*in a deep, horrific voice*): I come for you.
PUNCH *faints away on the stage.*

A deep shudder ran through Alice as she rehearsed the scene
again. That horrid croaking voice was hardly her own. And
with each repetition, as Punch grew ever more convincingly
terrified, the Devil grew stronger, sapping his strength, insid-
iously sucking the life from him. And simultaneously the
Devil was sucking her own life into itself as well, leaving her
a hollow shell.

Yet she could not stop; something had awakened that
would not let her stop. Soon all thought of the script lay far
behind. The lines were living now—spoken spontaneously,
terrifyingly real. As real as were her despairing cries at the
close of the play as the Devil bore her off on his back.

23

TIME PASSED. THE DOLLS AT THE
table sat woodenly before the remnants of their tea.
The sun had fled the window, leaving those against
the wall in shadow. They too had turned to shells.

There was a sudden sound. From somewhere infinitely
far off she heard her name being called. A small arm
appeared, pushing the puppets down, forcing them from the
stage. The dialogue ran on for a moment by itself, then fal-
tered, failed. Her arms fell leadenly to her sides.

She caught sight of herself in the glass. Her hair was
drenched with perspiration. Her face was drawn, ghostly
white, her eyes etched with exhaustion. Her arms felt as if
they might fall off.

She looked down and saw Lela standing silently in front
of her. The puppets dropped with a dull thud to the floor at
her feet.

Lela led her over to the bottom bunk and laid her down
among the dolls. Then she ran from the room. She returned
with Aunt Emily in tow.

"Good Lord, Alice, what's wrong?" She felt Alice's forehead, went and dampened a cloth in the bathroom, folded
it, and laid it on her forehead. Then she took the mirror
down and picked the puppets up off the floor. She stood
for what seemed a long while, looking down at the Devil in
her hand.

"Put it away," said Lela, lingering in the doorway. "It's
bad. It's very bad."

157

At her insistence the puppets were once again tucked safely away in the book bag.

Alice remained in bed for the rest of the day, ministered to by Lela as diligently as if she were an ailing doll. She covered her with an assortment of blankets borrowed from the doll things, took her temperature with the toy thermometer from her doctor's kit, listened gravely for her heartbeat with the plastic stethoscope that squeaked.

Alice drifted in and out of sleep. From time to time Aunt Emily would peek in and ask if she needed anything. The consensus seemed to be that she would live.

Evening came. The house filled with shadows. Lights were switched on against the onset of night. At one point Alice awoke, after yet another brief, disorienting sleep, to find herself alone in the room. The desk lamp had been turned on; so too the fan. She felt chilled. Her book bag had disappeared from the chair. The events of the afternoon were a blur.

She could hear the murmur of conversation in the kitchen below, Father's voice carrying above the rest. She lay for a while listening, staring dully up at the framework of boards supporting the upper bunk, aware of a curious cramping low down in her abdomen. She felt as though she might be sick.

It was with a sudden sense of urgency that she sat up, stood on limp legs, and made her way to the bathroom. Ten minutes later she reemerged, visibly pale, and took herself silently down the hall to Mother's room.

She was back in her own bunk when Lela came to bed. She was dimly aware of Father feeling her forehead and pulling the sheets up around her shoulders, dimly aware of Lela leaning down to kiss her, settling one of the stuffed dolls in beside her under the sheets. Then oblivion.

At some point in the night she had a dream. She dreamed that she and Lela were in the woods behind the house along with Asha and two of the other inside dolls. The doll table and chairs had been set up among the trees, and Lela was serving them all tea. She had filled the teapot with the sludgy water from the stream and was pouring the brown liquid happily into the tiny plastic cups while she chattered away.

The unsettling aspect of the dream was that Alice herself had become no more than a doll. She sat perched precariously on the tiny chair, utterly unable to move. Her arms dangled slackly by her side. A large hump had formed on her back, which forced her to lean forward and rest her full weight against the edge of the table to keep from toppling over.

She was completely aware of everything that was going on, but absolutely incapable of communicating. There was an overwhelming terror in this, coupled as it was with the awareness that the other dolls were equally alive, but resigned to their state. The Victoria doll seemed especially pleased to see her in such desperate straits, as if in retribution for the indignity she herself had suffered in being shut away in the shed.

Lela moved happily from each to each, lifting their cups and coaxing the rusty brown liquid between their lips, blissfully oblivious of its drooling down their chins and onto their clothes. She lifted the tiny cup and tipped its contents between Alice's lips. Alice felt her mouth fill up with the foul water, felt it drain disgustingly down her throat. The dolls looked on with wide unblinking eyes.

Asha was sitting next to her, her stiff rubber arms held uselessly in front of her, while Lela fed tea into the bottle hole punched between her puckered lips. Alice watched in horrid fascination as the dark brown liquid drained from the hole between the doll's legs, pooling on the chair.

Lela busied herself now with making dinner, crumbling dead leaves onto the plastic plates in front of them. There was not quite enough to go around. She bent down to scoop up another handful. It was then Alice noticed the birds.

They were sitting motionless on the branches of the trees about them, ranged in silent rows, staring; each one the image of the next, as though cut from one pattern. Patterned too were the trees, hardly trees at all now, but thick vertical stalks like bars, closely spaced, with broad flat leaves branching from them. Beyond lay darkness, deep and foreboding.

Instantly Alice was aware she was in a dream. The pattern was that on the wall by the bed. Its shadows, she knew, were not empty. Even now she could hear the light rustle of leaves, see the startling blackness of the birds' eyes as they nervously plumbed the darkness beyond.

Momentarily it would appear. She would feel the awful presence that moved behind the pattern, patiently testing the space between the stalks, seeking a way out. She tried to wake herself, to force herself to move. But she could no more break the grip of nightmare than she could budge from the table where she sat, a doll among dolls.

Lela carefully crumbled the dead leaves onto a plate and pushed them over in front of her. Alice begged her with her eyes to turn around, to see before it was too late the thing that even now began to take shape between the trees. Lela smiled, lifted a spoonful of leaves, and coaxed them between her lips.

And again Alice saw those two fierce eyes burning in the shadows. They drew steadily nearer, until first the outline and then the features of a face imprisoned in the pattern took shape. A lean white face leered out at her, ravenous as a wolf. And she knew that it had finally found the way out.

Terror shot through her like an electric shock. Her limp body stiffened; she felt herself lurch away from the table edge and begin to slowly topple sideways off the chair. She was aware of falling, falling it seemed forever, aware of Lela looking dumbly on, aware of the figure pushing free of the pattern behind her. As her head hit the ground she awoke.

She shot up in the bed, her heart hammering violently. Her eyes raced frantically over the pattern on the wall. Nothing troubled its calm.

Over the whir of the fan, she heard the sound of Lela snoring. Then something caught her eye—the limp strap of the book bag trailing from beneath the blanket at the foot of her bed.

24

"TWO VANILLA CONES, PLEASE."
The shop owner gave Emily a look that verged on recognition, then let his old eyes flit away. They settled on Lela.

"Aren't you a lucky young lady?" he said as he slid open the lid of the ice-cream cooler and reached down into the tub with the scoop.

Lela nodded and even managed a shy smile as he handed her the heaping cone. It was the first glimmer of light Emily had seen from her all day. Something clearly was troubling her; she had not even wanted to be read to. Finally, in an effort to coax her out, Emily had suggested the walk.

The shop owner handed her the other cone, noticeably smaller, and closed the cooler. Again there was that faint glimmer of recognition in his eyes.

Was it possible that he really did recognize her? It had been more than twenty-five years since she'd been in this store. Way back when her brother Albert was a baby she had often stopped here for ice cream when she was out walking him.

She had been stunned today to see the place still standing, looking as if it had been only yesterday since she'd wheeled Albert in his rusty stroller up to its door. Even the inside was the same: stuffed toys suspended on wires from the ceiling, dolls watching through the dusty plastic windows of their boxes on the shelves, comics ranged in rows on the rack, candy bars in open boxes by the counter.

It should have been comforting that while so much of

the past had fallen into oblivion, this place remained unchanged. It *should* have been comforting; instead it was somehow terrifying. For it brought the dread reality of that lost summer back with a sudden, savage force, as though piece by piece the curtain of time were crumbling away.

She fumbled through her pockets for the correct change and handed it to the old man behind the counter. Time had touched him with the same dusty hand as it had the dolls on their forgotten shelves.

"It's been a long time," he said shockingly as he took the money from her, dropping it into the till.

"Yes," she agreed, "a long time."

"Your daughter?" He nodded toward Lela, who had wandered out front with her ice cream.

"Yes," she found herself saying, without so much as a moment's pause.

"Cute as a button, isn't she?"

"Yes, she's a little sweetheart all right."

Outside, as they began to walk away from the store, she pictured the old man staring out the window after them. Mother and daughter. Was it wicked of her to have lied, to have allowed herself the brief delight of fantasy?

It seemed to her now that her entire life had been shaped by fantasies of a darker sort. Had she been spared, her life might well have taken a different course. She could well be walking down this sunlit street with a real daughter by her side, instead of one that faded from her as quickly as the ice cream melted in the cone.

How simple, how wonderful it would have been, never to have been touched by terror. And yet she could never truly wish it otherwise, for all that she was took root in that soil. Had it not been for that summer, for the utter change it

163

had wrought in her, she would never have written a word; there would have been no need. And she would not wish that away for the world. No, she had been set apart—set apart to watch, to wait, to write. She only prayed she would be ready, when the time was ripe, to act.

They walked silently along the empty street, Emily lost in her thoughts, Lela in her ice cream. She had eaten it down to a tiny thimble of cone when Emily looked up and found they were standing in front of the town house development.

In former days, when it had been the Bedford Ravine, it and the depot nestled near its edge on the far side of the bridge had been the last landmark on their walks home. It had been on one such walk that Albert had run off into the depot that day.

Today she had instinctively retraced the same route with Lela. She stood now momentarily numbed by the dreadful irony of it all. Her whole life it seemed led here. She was only dimly aware of Lela tugging on her arm.

"Can we go to the park, Aunt Emily?" she pleaded. "Please?"

"Of course we can, love," she said distractedly, then watched in horror as Lela darted away from her and ran off down the street.

"Wait!" she cried. "Where are you going?" But Lela had already disappeared around the corner.

She ran after her, following the curve of the wall that fronted the town houses, rounding the corner onto Bedford Avenue. Ahead of her lay the level crossing. The arm of the gate was raised as if in alarm. The street was empty. There was not a sign of Lela.

She ran shouting alongside the wall toward the tracks. A

car crawled past. The driver leaned out and looked at her as if she were mad. A flock of pigeons, feeding from the garbage bins behind the building, took to the air in a startled flurry. The air rang with the leathery slap of their wings.

The bins stood against the blank back wall of the building at the entrance to a narrow dirt alley. The smell that poured through them now though was not the smell of garbage. It was the dark seductive odor of damp soil and leaf mold, the smell that had pervaded the ravine that stood here those many years ago. It was as if the ravine, awakened from its long sleep, was arising now. The entire scene seemed on the verge of dissolving into green.

At that moment she heard the sound of a swing. It came from somewhere down the lane, a slow rhythmic creaking, like the labored breathing of some creature of steel. She followed it as she might have followed a frail strand of thread leading her through a maze. She had the sense that it was taking her back through time.

The chain link fence that bordered the lane on one side was wound with morning glories, their purple trumpet flowers raised in a silent flourish. Beyond lay the track and the rusted roadbed.

The creaking of the swing grew louder, until the alley ended and she found herself suddenly in a small open area of scrub grass and weeds, bordered on three sides by the back of the project and on the fourth by the fence. It struck her with a strange force of unreality, for in all the times she'd visited the project, she'd had no notion it was there.

In the midst of the space stood a massive electrical tower; in its shadow, a small playground, bordered by a low iron fence. There, pumping herself back and forth on a set of swings, sat Lela.

The playground was a bleak, abandoned thing—a set of monkey bars, a sandbox, two wooden teeter-totters, and the swings. All were in poor repair, badly in need of painting, stamped by the obvious signs of neglect. The park had obviously been intended to serve the needs of the project. It appeared to have failed.

Lela saw her coming and smiled happily over at her.

"You shouldn't have run off like that," said Emily, a sudden surge of anger welling up in the wake of relief. "I didn't know where you were." She tramped through sand and wood chips toward the swing.

"But you said we could go."

"Yes, but I didn't know there was a playground here. How did you?"

"Alice brought me."

"Alice? When?"

"Last week."

Last week. It could have meant anything. Last week, last month, last year. But why should Alice bring her here?

"Push me, Aunt Emily."

Lela leaned back into the arc as the swing scooped into the sky, then hunched forward as it fell back. The power lines hummed overhead. Danger 10,000 Volts, read the sign bolted to one of the iron legs of the electrical tower.

Its massiveness dwarfed them. High overhead it held the hissing wires aloft like snakes in its metal arms. And in the near distance stood another, and another, stationed like monstrous steel sentries along the desolate swath of railway land that cut the town in two. She thought of the one she could see from her window, brooding over the woods. They seemed to her now the image of that implacable power that hung poised over all their heads.

She pushed the child skyward again into the heart of the hum. As she glanced about, a sudden chill ran through her; the swing flew back and almost struck her in the face. From the position of the tower and the track she suddenly realized she could determine where the old depot had been. In fact it had stood on this very site.

Here then was the heart of the maze. How strange that after all her looking it should be Lela that led her here.

Lela soon grew tired of the swing. The slide was useless, sticky with something that had been spilled from the top and allowed to ooze down the length of it. She scrambled halfheartedly up the monkey bars, but the joy that had come briefly with the cone had gone out of her again.

She settled on the edge of the sandbox, found a paper cup, and ran to rinse it at the open spigot of the water fountain. She came back with it filled to the brim, splashing gouts of water onto the ground.

Emily sat on the edge of the sandbox. It too was a wreck, bristling with shards of glass, wads of weathered paper, cigarette butts. She sifted through the sand with a stick, plucking out the garbage, gathering it in a pile against the inside of the box. As she worked she looked around, scanning the backs of the buildings. She had the strange sensation of being watched.

Lela squatted beside her in a patch of sand she had already cleared. She hollowed out a shallow hole with her hand, banked the sand about its edges, then emptied the cup of water into it. Before it drained away into the sand, she collapsed the bank on top of it, making mud. She smoothed a place in the sand in front of her, scooped out the sand, and began to shape a figure from it.

The wires buzzed like hornets overhead. Emily scraped

compulsively with the stick, scratching like a claw at the crusted sand, unearthing still more bits of broken glass: danger, lurking just below the surface. She had a sudden clear and overpowering picture of the two of them sitting in this filthy sandbox, trying to wring some momentary joy from this site of desolation.

Lela was muttering to herself as she worked. "It was bad. The puppet was bad."

"Yes, dear." But Emily was only half listening. For from the heart of the hum she suddenly heard a voice, a voice as familiar to her as nightmare.

Come along, sweetheart, don't be bashful. There's nothing to be afraid of. The professor won't bite.

A chill ripple raced down her spine.

"I could hear it talking," Lela went on. "It said wicked things. Wicked. I wanted it to go away."

"Yes. Yes, dear." But she was still not listening. There was sharp pain in her palm. When she looked she noticed needlelike thorns bristling along the length of the stick she held in her hand. It was a branch from a rosebush. Her eyes flew up and swept around the playground. Rising from the soil at the base of one leg of the tower was a large rosebush. It seemed to her now that the pattern of the branches wound about the steel struts had assumed a human shape, a skeletal figure shackled to the tower. The bush was dead; there was not so much as a single bloom upon it. Yet for one mad moment Emily swore there was a smell of roses in the air.

The sound that came from the top of the tower was like a laugh. She glanced up. Birds had settled in the metal ribs of the beast. Clouds scudded past, making it momentarily appear that the tower was toppling.

"It made Alice sick," said Lela. "It's bad. I wanted it to go away."

She was looking down at the figure she had shaped in the sand, a crude face with wide round eyes and a leering mouth. Two horns protruded from the top.

"The puppet couldn't really make Alice sick," said Emily. "It's just pretend; it's not real." But her assurances sounded hollow even to herself. There was an almost palpable sense of menace in the air. She had to get Lela away.

"No. No, it wasn't pretend," insisted Lela. "It was bad. Bad." And she smashed the mud figure with her hand, scattering sand over the box.

"We'd better go," said Emily, taking Lela's muddy hand and walking quickly away from the playground with her, eager for the safety of the street.

As they started down the lane she turned and took one last look back at the tower. For a mad moment she could have sworn that a lean figure stood there in the shadows, smiling back at her.

Alice took the long way to the library that afternoon. In the wake of her dream, the prospect of walking through the woods filled her with dread. She made her way quickly down the street, already late for work. Her book bag bounced lightly against her back, like the insistent prodding of some unseen presence urging her on.

She was blind to the life about her; people passed like shadows cast against an inner screen on which a nightmare scene replayed itself repeatedly.

She felt a terrible urgency to be rid of the puppets. As she turned through the iron gate of the library her eye was drawn to the row of stone birds that formed the brackets below the eaves of the building. It seemed to her now that they had shifted slightly in the night so that, like the birds in the wallpaper pattern, one eye was fixed upon her while the other was busy with something within.

She kept her eyes glued to the ground as she came up the stairs, refusing like Lela to let her eyes wander to the arch above the doorway, where the gargoyle glared silently down through the leaves.

25

EACH EVENING FOR THE FOLLOWING
week Emily returned to the abandoned playground,
drawn as if by a magnet to the place. She would sit
on the bench, with her book on her lap, pretending to read.
Inwardly, though, she sat in anxious vigil before a darkened
depot on the edge of a deep ravine.

The events of that terrifying summer twenty-eight years
ago sprang up in memory with numbing clarity now, striking
her with a force almost physical. Words on the page gave
way to images drawn from that night. And more than once
she caught herself glancing up, momentarily shocked to find
the deteriorating town house project clapped down like a
sudden lid on the site.

It was twilight now, the hour of anxiety, that dangerous
borderland between day and dark. She sat on the bench,
straining to read. But the words had turned liquid, pooling
in inky puddles on the page. Around her she felt the inex-
orable fall of dark, the quiet bleeding of color from the
earth.

Once night fell she would be fine. Then terror too
would drain away; there would be refuge in the invisibility of
darkness. It was now that she felt utterly vulnerable, when
the laws of daylight no longer held true and the world was in
the grip of dream. If there were demons, this was the hour in
which they would awaken, this the hour in which they would
pass unhindered into the world.

As she sat in the uncertain light, the steady hum of the
power lines atop the tower was the magician's lilting voice,

droning in her ear. She could picture him as plainly as if he stood before her now: his pallid flesh, his piercing eyes, that low, melodious voice. The sandbox became his stage; ghost children sat upon the ground before it; and he performed the show as he had that night.

The soil was steeped in memory. Yet as the days went by, a doubt had begun to root itself in her mind—and with it a hope. What if these memories were themselves illusions— hollow, ultimately harmless—merely the shell of something long since dead, as dead as the rosebush wrapped about the tower? What if, after all, he were not here? What if the shadows were all that remained?

A burst of laughter broke the silence. It came from the direction of the town houses. She glanced up and saw three lean figures leap the low brick wall behind one of the houses. A chill ran through her.

She could not make out their features in the failing light. They strutted in the studied manner of young men, smoke trailing in their wake, a bottle passing among them. Instantly she understood that this was their destination, this was their bench. These were the children to whom the park had fallen. The butts and broken bottles in the sand were their discarded toys.

They were nearly as far as the fence before they saw her sitting there. They stopped in their tracks and stared.

They inspired fear. It was their intent to inspire fear. She was in battle with spirits. This sudden menace of flesh and blood unnerved her. She briefly met their gaze, then looked back to her book. The words washed like rainwater down the gutter of the page, leaving a white emptiness in their wake.

At the touch of terror time dissolved. Her clothes seemed suddenly too large; her legs no longer touched the ground. And she was sure that what these boys saw now in the dream-ridden twilight was not a grown woman at all, but a frightened girl of fourteen.

Truly time was an illusion. In the face of fear or wonder all times were one. Layer upon layer upon layer.

Over the fence they came. She glanced up at them again. They were close enough now that she could see their faces. They were so young. Little boys in leather, so desperate to be grown.

She closed the book and folded her hands upon it. For a moment she thought they might pounce, but as they stood there staring, a silence fell upon them, their resolve seemed to evaporate, and finally they swaggered off across the sand, laughing among themselves. One of them looked back once and shook his head. As they passed the swings he took one and flung it fiercely into the air. It circled the crossbeam and hurtled down like a hung man dropped through the trap. They retreated to the shadows near the lane and by degrees grew one with the darkness. Only the bright embers of their cigarettes betrayed them there. She sensed they would be back.

She yearned desperately for a cigarette. She ransacked her bag in vain, felt through all her pockets twice in hopes of turning up a stray; there were none.

She clutched her Shakespeare on her lap as though it were a talisman to ward off evil. It had been a gift from Miss Potts. She could still remember her reading aloud from it those long years ago, could still feel the spell the words cast as she spoke. Dear Miss Potts. She could almost sense her sitting beside her here on the bench in the dark, feel her thin hand alight gently on her own, hear her words in the depot that day so long ago.

All we can do is wait and watch, and hope that, when the night draws near again, there will be someone left who remembers the last time and is ready for him.

"Someone like me," she whispered to the dark.

Yes, my dear, someone like you.

But I have waited, she told herself. I have watched and waited. What if we were wrong?

An hour flew by. She had the disquieting sense that time could no longer be trusted. Back home they would be beginning to worry. How odd after all these years to be living in a place where people actually worried about her.

It was after eleven when she heard the approach of a train: the distant whistle, the urgent gong of the bell as the gate lowered at the level crossing, the sudden rush of steel and shuttered light, faces framed in windows instantly whisked away; shadows passing in the dark.

In a week—oh, in a week, God willing—all this too would be past, all this long anxiety would be over. And perhaps nothing would have happened. Perhaps, in the end, they had been wrong. Yes, and she would feel ridiculous for a while. Ridiculous. But then she would start to put her life together again. The baby would be along soon. Yes, and Elizabeth could use her help for a while. She would have to move, of course. But there would be someplace she could live, something she could do to make a little money. Somehow she would manage; she always had. There were people to repay, debts to be settled. There was so much to do; and so much time had been wasted on terror. Soon it would end.

26

ALICE SAT IN THE DARKENED kitchen, her housecoat wrapped about her. The *Wonder Book* lay like a shadow on the table before her. Her finger traced the letters of the title tooled in the cover, like one adrift in some impossible maze.

Again she glanced at the clock. It was after twelve. Still there was no sign of Aunt Emily. Her eye fell on the calendar taped to the side of the fridge, and a thin whisper of terror ran through her.

She had the sense that this solid-seeming world was now as liquid as a dream. It could shift, meld, metamorphose before her eyes; at any moment something utterly impossible might occur. As her finger traced the title on the book of fairy tales, she felt like one cast headlong into its world.

It was at the library she felt it most. The very bricks seemed to breathe. The pattern in the marble moved, like oil on water. On the wall of the Children's Room the shadows in the mural had deepened; she imagined she saw a lean figure lurking among the painted trees.

Time and again she found herself drawn instinctively up the winding stair to the forgotten display cases on the second floor, to read the flier for a magic show and stare down into the face of a girl in a photograph.

Something was poised to happen. She could feel it now, feel it with every fiber of her being. And it frightened her more than anything had ever frightened her in her life.

On Monday she had barely come through the door before Mr. Dwyer whisked the puppets away from her and hurried off downstairs. Later she found him in his office, fingering the scar on the devil's forehead as if he were tending a wounded child.

She could hardly bear to be near him now. There was an unclean smell about him, a smell of smoke and sweat that made her stomach turn.

He must have sensed it. He had not even bothered to ask her once this week to stay late to practice the show. Her relief at not having to crowd into the cramped confines of the puppet theater with him was overshadowed by the mounting panic she felt. With the show scheduled for Saturday, they were still far from ready. Not once had they run through the closing scene together. It was almost as if he were saving it for the performance itself.

Twelve-fifteen. Where could Aunt Emily be? Yet Alice knew full well where she had gone tonight, where she had gone every night for weeks now. She had even followed her one evening, walking Lela past the entrance to the town houses where her aunt had disappeared, stumbling upon a playground at the rear of the place. She had stood there pushing Lela on the swings, thinking to herself, This is insane. This whole thing is completely insane.

The fridge gave a loud click and shut itself off. In the sudden silence she heard the sound of footsteps on the porch, a slight rattle of the handle as the key slid home, a quiet creak as the door edged open and Emily came in.

She started when she saw Alice standing in the kitchen doorway.

"What on earth are you doing up?" she whispered.

"I couldn't sleep. I was worried about you."

Emily fixed her for a moment with those unreadable eyes. She sloughed off her coat and draped it over the newel post.

"You'd better get along to bed."

"I can't. I have to talk to you."

"I'm very tired, Alice. Can't it keep till morning?"

"No. No, it can't."

The kettle rocked gently on the red coils of the burner as it came to a boil. The stove light fell on the two figures seated in semidarkness at the kitchen table. The clock crept toward one.

Emily had disappeared briefly upstairs, then quietly returned with a sweater over her shoulders and a cigarette in her hand. She struck a match and lit it. In the momentary glare of the match Alice saw a face etched with exhaustion. Then the match was out and they were cast in shadow again.

The kettle shrieked. She ran to quiet it, made two coffees, and brought them back to the table. They sat sipping in silence. The hand that held the cigarette shook. The smell of the smoke cast Alice back to that day in the car.

You're not going to believe a word of what I'm going to tell you. No more than I did when I was told. But it's true. Every single word of it—I swear.

"Where were you tonight?" asked Alice; her hands toyed nervously with the book.

Emily exhaled a weary stream of smoke, stared down at the table a long while before answering. "I think you know." It was like pulling words up one by one from a deep well. "What was it you wanted to talk to me about?"

Alice felt so utterly alone, so utterly lost and frightened and alone. She would have given anything to bridge the impossible chasm between them, to somehow connect. Tears came before she could even try to stop them.

"I'm sorry. Oh God—I didn't mean to do this." She brushed them away with the back of her hand.

Emily stubbed out the cigarette. She leaned across the table, took the hand that plucked at the frayed binding and covered it with hers.

Alice looked at their hands joined together on the book. She suddenly realized it was the first time they had touched. Closing her eyes, she let the words come. She talked about the library, the foreboding she felt there, the aura of menace that seemed to envelop the building. She spoke of Mr. Dwyer and the change that had come over him since they'd decided to do the Punch-and-Judy show, the growing sense of unease she felt around him.

"Then tonight, something happened. I was getting ready to leave, and I went to get my coat from the workroom. I found him there working at the table. He had taken down all the signs for the show. He said he had decided to postpone it. We weren't nearly ready yet; we needed more time. He was pasting strips of paper with the new date to each of the signs." She stopped and looked her aunt full in the face.

"Aunt Emily, the new date is Saturday, August eighth."

The hand that held hers instantly turned to stone.

The fan was on in the girls' room. Emily knew better than to turn it off. Lela, who drifted on the very surface of sleep, would awaken at once. She tiptoed quietly across the room, closed the window, locked it. For a minute she stood looking out at the ragged silhouette of woods. In the distance, the electrical tower loomed above the treetops, skeletal, sinister. Behind it lay the dark dome of the library. She clutched her sweater about her as if to ward off some wakening chill.

She stole over to the bunk beds, pulled the covers up around Lela's shoulders, and leaned down among the dolls to kiss her lightly on the cheek. Lela threw an arm around her neck and murmured, "I love you, Mommy" in her sleep.

"I love you too, sweetheart," she whispered back.

Alice was lying on her back in the upper bunk. Her breath came in deep rhythmic waves. Emily kissed her own hand and touched it lightly to Alice's forehead.

"Forgive me," she said and crept quietly from the room.

With the click of the door, Alice opened her eyes, turned, and cautiously plumbed the patterned wall.

Back in her room, Emily lay down on the sleeping bag. The candle burned by her side. The bars of the crib were cast in shadow on the ceiling, a cage in which her mind raced around frantically.

Was it mere coincidence that this puppet show should fall on the very day? Or was it more? No, she told herself time and again, it was all wrong. The place was utterly wrong. Yet she remembered clearly the feeling of dread that had come upon her that day in the library when she had found the knife, the sense that if she simply turned she would find the magician there as well. She had taken it for memory then. Could it have been more?

The depot no longer existed. All that remained of what it once held was housed in a scattering of display cases against a library wall. Could it be that, along with the dusty travel posters and faded photographs, the power that had clung to that old place had been transported there? Had it lain there like one dead, quietly encased in glass, alongside a flier for a magic show and a mysterious knife, only waiting for the hour of its awakening?

Each time she closed her eyes she was back in the playground again, staring at the tower, hearing the mocking drone of the magician's voice. Suddenly she had the dreadful conviction that he had been toying with her as she sat there night after night, mocking her with memories, reducing her to a child sitting spellbound in the dark, like those children that night at the show. And all the time he was elsewhere.

Truly he was a master of illusion. He spun deception the way a spider spins its web. She trembled before his power, a power as deadly and seductive as the electricity that sang in the wires spun from tower to tower through town. How could she ever hope to defeat him?

But a puppet show? How was it possible? It was a magic show she had seen that night. Professor Mephisto had been a magician.

As she lay there staring at the dance of shadows on the ceiling she thought of Lela's fear of the puppet figure, her belief that it had made Alice sick. She had tried to tell the child that it was only her imagination. But where in the end did imagination leave off and reality begin? She had lost all sense of the borders between the two.

She fell at last into a fitful sleep. Again she was on the playground, sitting on the edge of the sandbox, the rose branch in her hand. It was twilight. The tower hissed and crackled overhead. And suddenly there was an overwhelming smell of roses in the air. She glanced down at her hand; the branch had broken into bloom.

It was then she saw the face in the sand. But now it was not a thing of mud at all. It was the gleeful white face of the magician glaring up at her, as if it were erupting from the grave.

Sometimes the dead do not stay buried.

Yet even as she watched, it began to change slowly, dying in the dying light. The flesh grew wooden, webbed with cracks, the mouth froze in a rictal grin, the eyes sank down to fiery stones. Two blackened horns broke through the skull. And she found herself staring at last into the leering face of the Devil puppet.

She awoke with a start, sprang bolt upright in the bed, chilled to the bone. The candle had guttered down to a pale flicker of flame in a puddle of wax. And it was as if the final piece in a puzzle had fallen into place.

"Mephisto," she whispered to the dark. "The magician's name was Professor Mephisto. Mephistopheles—the name of the Devil."

It was he. He had, as she had dreaded, struck when she least expected, from a direction she had not even imagined. All this time he had been right beneath her nose, and she too blinded by the past to see.

In a moment she understood it all. It was Alice he had settled on. It was she who was to be the assistant in the show now, as the children at the magic show had been before. And she, like them, would pay the deadly price.

In the terror of that moment the task was set. She knew that somehow she must destroy it, before it was too late. This was the task that had fallen to her. It was this she had been waiting for all these years. She prayed to God she had the strength to carry it through.

27

THE FOLLOWING SATURDAY, AUGUST 1, in lieu of the puppet show which had been promised, Parkview Public screened an old animated film. Mr. Dwyer had unearthed it from somewhere deep in the bowels of the basement, along with an ancient projector still in working order. The crowd was considerable; in addition to the ragtag bunch of neighborhood children who gravitated to the library for want of anything better to do, several uptown parents with a fondness for puppets had appeared with their children. They craned their necks to admire the stained-glass dome, ran their hands along the marble railing, with the air of tourists traveling abroad. One sensed it was for their sake the film had been found.

Alice was on duty at the main desk, while Mr. Dwyer, looking decidedly ill, sat in the Children's Room under cover of darkness, running the projector. As there was no door to the room, the din of the soundtrack reverberated through the building. The library, sunk quietly in its hundred-year-old haze, was receiving a shock from which it might never recover.

They had just begun the second reel. By now the noise had sent most of the adult patrons scurrying to the remote corners of the building. The old gentleman working on his local history project in the upstairs room appeared periodically at the railing of the rotunda to squint down at the darkened room and shake his head.

A large cardboard box sat on the counter. A young woman, deeply tanned, her sunglasses pushed to the top of her head, had dropped if off a few minutes before. The box was full of books. They had obviously been to the beach; as Alice removed the cards from their pockets and sorted the books on the cart, sand sifted down to the floor at her feet.

Sunlight filtered down through the stained-glass dome in the ceiling. Flecks of colored light quivered on the countertop. She glanced up. For the first time the pattern seemed to resolve itself into a picture. She saw a wooden trellis wound with roses. Then, at the center of the scene, a scarlet eye.

It was the very image of the Devil's jeweled eye. For a terrifying moment she sensed the horrid thing hovering inexorably over them all.

As she loaded the last of the books onto the cart she leaned forward over the counter and peered into the dimness of the Children's Room. She could just see a corner of the makeshift screen and beyond it the sunlit outline of the alcove windows, their shades drawn down.

Neither Mr. Dwyer nor the projector was in her line of sight. She had no idea how much of the film remained. Nonetheless, she turned now from the counter and made her way quickly past Mr. Dwyer's office and down the hall. Her legs had turned liquid with apprehension.

She stopped at the supply closet at the end of the hall by the workroom door. The bulb had blown. She rooted around in semidarkness until she found a dustpan and a broom to sweep up the sand. If Mr. Dwyer were suddenly to appear, these would be her excuse for being absent from the desk.

As she closed the closet door she caught the faint odor of cigarette smoke in the hall. The talk in the kitchen three nights before flashed through her mind, then sudden panic as she studied the closed door of the workroom and wondered if Mr. Dwyer could possibly have ducked in there for a smoke without her seeing him go by. She reached out and nudged the door with the end of the broom. It swung open listlessly and banged against the rubber stopper with a soft dead thud.

The room, of course, was empty. It smelled of smoke and coffee and the greasy remains of food. Dirty dishes covered the counter, along with empty containers from the all-night place across the street. The red light glowed on the coffeemaker; the pot sat stained and empty beside a saucer full of butts. Half a dozen roses drooped in a jar.

There was an aura of corruption to the scene. She felt like gathering up the rotting garbage, rinsing the dishes in the sink, setting them back in ordered rows upon the shelf. But she dared not. There was no telling how he would take it. He was set like a hair trigger; the least disturbance might suddenly set him off.

Like an addict, he had ceased to care for anything but his addiction. It was terrifying to see. Today, as he stood in front of the screen to introduce the film, even the children had noticed there was something odd about him. All traces of the meticulously dressed young man had disappeared. His clothes had obviously been slept in; his mustache drooped limply over his lips. There was a haunted look about him, a sheen of madness in the sunken eyes; they had the glassy vacancy of one of Lela's dolls.

His hands seemed to have drawn from him whatever life he had left. They toyed incessantly with each other, ran agitatedly over his face, through his hair, sought escape yet found none.

He had closed his introduction of the film with the announcement that the Punch-and-Judy performance would take place the following Saturday. Pointing proudly to the refurbished puppet theater standing in the corner, he urged them all to attend this special children's show.

As he scurried to the back of the room, children turned and whispered to one another. The lights went down, and in the sudden darkness the film began.

Alice could just faintly hear the soundtrack now as she stood in the doorway of the room. With a quick glance back she crossed the room to the window, unlocked it, opened it a crack, and wedged a roll of tape between the sash and the windowsill. As she started back along the hall her heart hammered violently in her chest. She paused at the door of the archives room and peered in. The room was dark, but a light burned in the basement, illuminating the glass floor, casting in shadow the ragged crack that ran through the center panel. It seemed to her now like the luminous shell of some dark beast about to be born, and she, broom and dustpan in hand, the ridiculous caricature of a knight with sword and shield prepared to face the foe.

There was a faint flurry of applause, then a sudden stillness as the library settled back to its normal state. The film was over.

She made her way quickly back to the desk. The lights were on in the Children's Room. Already the first wave of kids had begun to file out. A couple of returns had been abandoned on the counter in her absence. She wondered whether a patron had rung the bell, and whether Mr. Dwyer perhaps had heard.

She began to sweep up the sand, keeping one eye fixed on the doorway, waiting for him to emerge. The sand had scattered everywhere. She had to pull out the book cart and sweep in behind. Finally she had it in a pile. The last of the kids had left; there was still no sign of Mr. Dwyer.

As she bent down to sweep it up her eye was drawn to

the office behind her. Miss Witherspoon peered down from the wall at her. Boxes of puppet shows were stacked below her portrait like offerings set before a shrine. The expression on her face, which she had taken once for severity, now looked like fear.

From the dimness of the Children's Room there came a sound of voices, a high shrill voice she recognized at once and then a croaking, hardly human sound that sent a shiver up her spine. Punch and the Devil played out their final scene.

Emily sat on the floor by the bunks reading to Lela from the *Wonder Book*. She had just given her a bath and washed her hair. As she listened, Lela leaned her damp head against Emily's blouse; the delicate scent of shampoo perfumed the air.

The dolls sat ranged about them on the rug. Asha, as always, seemed out of place—stiff and strange, her clothes, though new, not quite right still, a startled look lingering in the eye that would not close. She was the wounded one; it had made her somehow more real than the rest, as if in some way she were blessed by brokenness.

The story was "The Nightingale," one of the milder stories in the collection. As she read it, Emily took brief refuge from the terror she felt closing around her in the sure rhythm of the words rolling off her tongue and the pictures they made in her mind.

Lela, too, succumbed to the spell; her mouth fell open; her eyes stared unseeing toward the corner of the room, while other, inward eyes opened. She sat as spellbound as the dolls around them. How strange, thought Emily, that symbols on a page could weave such magic. She would never grow used to the mystery of it.

From time to time as she read, her eyes would dart suddenly to the door or come to rest on the clock upon the dresser. She expected Alice to arrive home at any moment, had been expecting her at any moment since she began getting Lela ready for bed over half an hour ago. She would not even permit the possibility that something had gone wrong to enter her mind.

As they neared the end of the story, where the nightingale returns from exile just in time to charm Death itself from the bed of the emperor with its song, there was a soft click of the door, and Alice looked in. Their eyes met, and with a slight bob of her head Alice showed she had succeeded in her purpose. Emily began to breathe again.

But her relief was short lived; all too soon it was displaced by the specter of the task that lay ahead. Long after the story was over, and Lela, with a quick peck on her cheek, had climbed into bed, Emily sat alone on the floor among the dolls, the damp spot on her blouse feeling cold against her skin as the shadows slowly deepened in the room.

It was after eight when Father arrived home. Emily and Alice had arranged to go to a movie together once he got in. They left shortly before nine, telling him not to bother waiting up. As he headed up the stairs to see Mother, he briefly wondered why.

Meanwhile, the car threaded through the narrow night streets. It made its way to the Palace Theater, a run-down rep house not far from the housing project. They bought their tickets from a young man in a T-shirt, his hair tied back in a tail, then went and sat for two hours together in the dark. Afterward, neither would remember what film it was they watched.

28

ONLY ONE STORE ALONG THE STRIP
was still open, the all-night convenience place
across the street from the library. Its garishly lit interior stood in stark contrast to the darkness without. As they
pulled up to the curb in the car Alice glanced at the plastic
clock hanging in the window. The two hands hovered near
twelve. It was time.

Leaving the car was like launching out from the safety of
shore onto the churning swell of the sea. The doors closed
behind them with a terrifying finality. Alice sensed that the
last of the landmarks of civilization had been left behind,
that the realm they now entered stood under darker sway.

Aunt Emily walked noiselessly beside her, silent as a
shadow. She had not said so much as a word since they'd left
the theater. Her face was set like the frozen features of one
of Lela's dolls. Her eyes plumbed each shadow they
approached.

The street wore a different face in the dark. The road
had unaccountably narrowed. The gaunt, gabled buildings
lining the street seemed to lean inward on them like a stand
of ancient trees—sprouting brick branches, lacing their
crumbling limbs overhead until even the little light of the
moon was quenched by a canopy of stone. Faces fissured
open in their trunks to peer after the two figures hurrying
past. A sound like a leathery rustling of wings filled the air.

Alice reached out and took Aunt Emily's arm; it was as
though the two of them had wandered out of reality into the
dark world of Lela's *Wonder Book*—Hansel and Gretel adrift

in the magic wood. And up ahead in the clearing loomed the witch's cottage.

Two squat arabesque lampposts set to either side of the library property flung the spiked shadow of the fence onto the street. The gate in the fence had blown shut. Behind it the library slept. Not even the security lights that were normally left burning inside the building at night were on. The place stood in utter darkness, as though the cold red eye of the cupola, gazing onto the night, had mirrored within its marble walls the abyss above.

A car turned a corner and crept slowly toward them along the street—some creature of darkness, stalking prey. The beams of its headlights scooped the shadows before it. Alice felt the muscles in her aunt's arm tense as it approached. As it caught them in its cone of light it slowed, then slunk off into the night.

Aunt Emily took one last look down the empty street, then pushed open the gate and drew the two of them in. It swung shut with a loud clang behind them. As the sound died into silence Alice momentarily sensed the building stir, as if deep within it something had been roused from sleep. Her aunt seemed to sense it as well. Her eyes anxiously scanned the darkened facade: scrollwork ravens silvered by the moon, leering faces frozen in the stone.

"Let's go," she whispered. "You lead. I'll be right behind you. Don't use the flashlight unless you absolutely have to."

"Aunt Emily, I'm scared."

"Me, too."

Rather than keep to the path that ran beside the building and risk being seen, Alice led them in behind the rank row of bushes that grew close by the wall. They moved slowly, blindly feeling for branches in the dark, the leaf mold yielding beneath their feet like flesh. The air was hung with the same dark, secret smell that permeated the woods after rain, and Alice felt the awful echo of the fear she had felt there before.

The library loomed up beside them, sensed rather than seen, like a palpable darkness dwarfing them by its vastness. The building was no longer the sad relic the daylight would have it, housing the crumbling mementos of the past; it was now a thing of the night, as ancient as the ground from which it rose.

Finally they were free of the bushes and out in the open air again. The back of the library property stretched before them: the reflecting pool, reflecting nothing; beyond it the fence, the field, and finally the woods. There were no buildings now, no lights; only the skeletal silhouette of the electrical tower against a sky strewn with stars.

"Where now?" whispered Aunt Emily.

Alice pointed up at the row of windows set like wedges of blackness in the back wall of the building. Keeping close to the wall, she walked slowly along the grass, sensing volcanoes boiling beneath the sod. She glanced repeatedly at the shallow pit of the reflecting pool, trying to get her bearings. Beneath the fourth window she stopped and looked up.

"I think this is the one."

The concrete ledge that ran along the base of the window lay about eight feet off the ground. She hadn't realized it was so high.

Aunt Emily stood silent for a moment, looking at it looming above them; then she squatted to the ground. "Stand on my shoulders and I'll boost you up," she said. "Come on, it'll be all right."

Alice set one foot, then the other, on the narrow shoulders, then walked her hands up the wall as her aunt lifted her with seeming ease into the air.

She came chest high to the window ledge. She knew instantly it was the workroom window; flakes of old paint and stray cigarette butts littered the ledge. The window was open a crack; she could see the shadowed outline of the roll of tape.

She peered into the glass—and the abyss looked back. At first she saw nothing, nothing but unfathomable blackness. Then slowly a figure seemed to take shape among the shadows. And what she had at first taken for the reflection of the tower became a skeletal arm hung with rags, and peering out beneath it where her own reflection had been, the withered face of the witch pressed against the glass.

She pitched backward, almost losing her balance. But the shoulders supporting her stood firm as stone.

"Are you all right?" Aunt Emily whispered up.

"Yes," she lied, though the reflection was again her own.

"Can you get it open?

"I think so." She eased her hands under the sash and pushed up. The window slid open with alarming ease. The acrid odor of dust and stale cigarette smoke drifted out into the night, and with it a fleeting odor of something else—a dark cloying smell couched just below the surface. It touched her with the cold finger of terror, and suddenly she was more afraid than she'd ever been.

Aunt Emily must have sensed it, for without a word she lowered Alice to the ground. They stood looking up at the open window. To Alice it might have been the mouth of hell.

Her aunt took her by the shoulders. "Listen," she said, "you've done enough. Just tell me how I find the basement once I get inside. Then after you help me up, you can go."

"Not on your life. I'm not letting you go in there alone. If you're going, so am I."

There was no point in arguing.

"All right, then. Give me a boost. Once I'm in I'll pull you up after me."

Alice bent down and her aunt scrambled up onto her shoulders. She reached up, grabbed the window ledge, and pulled herself up, again with a seemingly effortless strength. Alice watched helplessly as she disappeared inside.

The instant she found herself standing in the room Emily knew she could not bring Alice in there with her. There was an unmistakable aura of malevolence about the place; she had the chill conviction that she had stepped irrevocably from the world of sense into another, infinitely darker world. It was the same sensation she'd had one night nearly thirty years ago, when she'd walked into the deserted depot—and out of time. Yet as it washed over her again now it was as if it had happened yesterday. That soft, musical voice sounded in her head.

Do come in, dear. Don't be shy. There's much more yet to come.

She stood stock still, shocked by the sheer force of it, not daring to budge. She felt beneath her sweater for the knife tucked in her belt. She prayed with all her heart that the power that clung to it still, once used for ill, might serve another purpose now. Panic pulsed through her in cold white waves. The whole of her life since that night had somehow been a preparation for this; and now she was suddenly not sure she could go through with it.

She heard Alice's urgent whispering from the darkness outside.

"Aunt Emily? Aunt Emily, is everything all right?"

She took a deep breath and leaned her head out the window.

"Alice, throw me up the flashlight and go back to the car."

"I can't. I won't."

"Go. I'll be all right, I promise you."

"But you don't know where to go."

"Then tell me."

"I'll *show* you. Just pull me up."

"No. Good-bye, Alice."

She drew her head in and quietly closed the window. It felt as if she were sealing herself inside a tomb. Underneath the smell of stale cigarette smoke and coffee there was another smell, darkly disturbing: a faint perfumelike odor that carried with it the undercurrent of decay, like flowers rotting on a grave.

She glanced around the room, making out the shadowy shapes of books on shelves, a counter with a coffeemaker, stray cups, a large table with a typewriter, more books. On the corner of the table nearest her was an ashtray, beside it a book of matches. She picked the matches up, struck one, and in the sudden flare of flame saw a doorway on the far side of the room and beyond it a hall. There were no other doors leading from the room. The way to the basement, wherever it was, lay somewhere beyond that door.

She had just started down the narrow hall when the match guttered out against her finger, plunging her instantly into darkness. She tried to light another, but terror turned her hands to blocks of ice, and the matchbook dropped uselessly to the floor.

She fell to her knees and began feeling about for it. The smell, now much stronger, was unmistakably that of roses. She remembered the sickening scent of them pervading the depot room that night. And again the magician's melodious voice sounded inside her, so clearly now that she felt he must be standing before her there in the darkness, that at any moment her groping fingers would fall on him.

Reality and illusion, which is which? Could it be, dear children, that life and death themselves are mere illusions?

It was not real, she tried to tell herself. It was only the memory of a voice, an echo of that night, sounding still.

Her hand closed over the matchbook; she tore out a match, struck it, and in its sudden, fragile light found herself alone in the hall. Imagination, that's how he works on you. He creeps into your imagination and twists it all in knots. He makes you see things that aren't there.

At the far end of the hall she could make out the vague outline of the main desk. A door to her left opened onto a supply closet. A sour-smelling mop stood in a pail. Her sense of smell had grown incredibly acute in the dark. It was smell that led her now to the open door on the right-hand side of the hall opposite the closet. For here the cloying odor was even more pronounced. She would have sworn the room was walled with flowers.

It was not. The flickering light of the match illuminated rather a room lined from floor to ceiling with books, very old books, many of them oversized and lying on their sides, their spines worn with age. The match burned quietly down and quenched itself against her flesh. She stood there in the dark, welcoming the pain, knowing that it alone now anchored her to the world. Her heartbeats reverberated against the walls.

Finally she lit another match and, turning, saw a wedge of darkness beyond the filing cabinets ranged against one wall. She made her way across the room with the dread inevitability of dream, until she stood before it. In the trembling light of the match she saw a narrow staircase leading down into the dark.

There was no use in calling with the window shut. Any noise she made would only put Aunt Emily more at risk. Alice made a few feeble attempts to jump up to the ledge, but it was utterly hopeless. She looked around for something she could stand on. It was hard to see much of anything in the dark. She began running alongside the back of the building, hoping to find something, anything. A terrible sense of foreboding grew inside her the longer Aunt Emily was alone in there, and no amount of reasoning would quiet it.

She had nearly come to the far corner of the building when she saw it. Snaking its limbs up a trellis set against the wall of the building was a rosebush, even in the dark obviously dead. She reached in behind it and gave the trellis a yank. It appeared to be anchored to the wall. She tried again, and this time it loosened, cracked, and suddenly came away from the wall, sending her sprawling onto the grass.

As she lay there looking up at the dark wall of the building, the rough sandstone blocks seemed to have smoothed themselves into sugar loaves. She thought of Gretel snapping off a bit of sugar candy to eat, and the shrill voice of the witch sounding inside the house.

As she scrambled to her feet a light winked on in the basement of the building.

29

COMING DOWN THOSE STAIRS WAS, to Emily, like descending, rung by desperate rung, into the dark recesses of herself. All the terrors she had struggled for so long to contain were waiting for her there. The cloying odor of roses, so strong upstairs, was overpowering here. It strove to mask another smell, a sharp musty smell, the smell of mildew and moldering books; to her, it was the smell of death. It was all she could do not to run.

The match light trembled down the stairs. They were like years, those stairs; she felt the child inside her slough them off as one by one they fell away. It was that child, finally, who stepped down onto a creaking wooden floor and found herself standing in the doorway of the depot waiting room.

A group of children sat in a semicircle on the floor. They twisted around to look at her, their faces white with light. Beyond them lay a makeshift stage: four squat barrels with planks laid across them.

On stage, the magician shook flowers from a paper cone, more flowers than the cone could possibly contain. The floor before the stage was strewn with roses. He stopped suddenly, shielded his eyes with his hand, and glanced out over the audience. "Well, well," he said, "I see a familiar face in the audience tonight. Do come in, dear. Don't be shy. There's much more yet to come."

She reached up and flicked a switch on the wall beside her. There was a furtive scrambling as of creatures darting into hiding, and a bulb dangling from the ceiling at the opposite end of the room winked into life.

There were no children; there was no stage, no magician—only an old wooden worktable, like the one her father had had in the basement of their bungalow back then. It sat in a pool of light cast by a bare bulb above it. Among random pots of paint and pieces of fabric, she saw four puppets lying face up in the light, like Lela's dolls tanning themselves on their towels. The one nearest her was dressed in black, the profile of its chalk white face terrifyingly familiar now. It was as if the magician standing on stage had withered himself playfully down to this.

It lay there silently, like a dead thing. But the terror mounting inside her screamed that it was not. She began to move toward the table, slowly, silently, as if not to awaken the wooden heads and limp cloth bodies that lay there under the light.

Boxes stacked in rows against the wall behind the table were like miniature caskets honeycombing a catacomb wall. Beyond the dim island of light surrounding the table, the shadows fell like a black backdrop over the rest of the basement. She stood in the center of the floor and peered hopelessly into them, sensing that they stretched out past the first faint shapes she could see into a darkness as deep as that which whirled forever above the world. She knew that if she were to wander into that darkness now, blindly searching for lights to ward it off, it would welcome her with waiting arms and she would never find her way back again.

She turned from it and fixed her eyes on the fragile globe of light above the bench. Her mind was full of music, the lilting music of the magician's voice.

Now, now, my dear. There's nothing to fear, nothing at all.

Again she saw him standing there on stage that night, those incredible eyes tunneling into her, exploring every corner and crevice of her, silencing all doubt, quietly shattering the lights of thought.

Now here she was, standing at a cluttered workbench in a library basement nearly thirty years later, staring into those same eyes again. Only now they were fixed like luminous stones in the painted face of a puppet. She felt as if at any instant they would swivel in their wooden sockets, the rigid smile would relax into flesh, and it would speak. The thought made her stomach pitch.

Come along, dear. Don't be shy.

The words sounded in her head as clearly as if they had been whispered in her ear. She felt a sudden, irresistible desire to slide her hand into the limp cloth body, to ease her fingers up into the hollow of its head, to give it life.

Could it be that life and death themselves are no more than illusions?

Yet some dim, desperate part of her screamed that if she did put her hand in there, her life would be instantly sucked from her and she would be overwhelmed with its own dark life.

She pulled her hand away, felt it brush against the hilt of the knife, clutching it the way a drowning man clutches at bits of wreckage. In some faint far-off part of herself she knew what she must do. She must bring the blade down with all her strength upon that smiling wooden head; she must hack the hideous thing to pieces, destroy it utterly.

Yet even as she moved to raise her hand her resolution wavered. Glancing down at the dead white face, it seemed to her suddenly that the blood red lips glistened in the light, as if they were wet.

She reached out one incredulous finger to touch them.

It came away red. A chill, reaming darkness spiraled up inside her.

Look at me. I said, look at me, girl.

The voice was no longer soothing, but cold, bloodless. Beneath it lay the unbridled fury of a wild beast. She could do nothing but obey. Her eyes locked helplessly onto his. A vast confusion enfolded her like a shroud.

And now those eyes *did* move in their wooden sockets, move with a cold mechanical smoothness until they settled full upon her. She felt her hand drawn inexorably toward the figure, felt the light kiss of the cloth against her fingers as they eased inside and edged upward toward the waiting hollow of its head.

And then from somewhere infinitely far off came the shrill sound of breaking glass. The spell was shattered for a moment, and in that moment she yanked her hand free of the puppet and brought the blade of the knife down sharply against its skull.

A startled look leaped into its eyes. Behind her, something stirred; a voice rang out.

"What are you doing there?"

She whirled and saw her father striding from the shadows toward her.

The rotted trellis had snapped twice under her weight as Alice tried to scale it to reach the workroom window. Now the splintered ends sank into the damp soil like knives as she wedged the toes of her shoes between the slats and pulled herself up.

She could just barely reach the ledge. The wood groaned beneath her weight. Somehow she would have to haul herself up onto the ledge from this position. She had the desperate sense that time was short.

She took a deep breath and launched herself off the trellis into the air, sensing even as she did so that it had sprung away from the wall and was standing upright in the darkness directly below her, bristling with spear points of shattered wood.

She had managed to haul herself up so that her arms were locked, her hands flat against the ledge, the upper half of her body above it. She could not bear the strain for long. Even now she felt her arms begin to buckle beneath her weight. Her feet scrabbled vainly for some sort of foothold in the wall. If she could only swing her legs onto the ledge. She had seen Emily do it—but the window had been open then. She would have to attempt it with the window closed, and somehow manage to keep her balance on the narrow ledge or risk being impaled on the broken trellis.

Her eyes searched desperately for something she could grab. They fell upon a hook protruding from the brick beside the frame about a foot above her head. With the last of her strength she swung her legs up onto the ledge and lunged for it.

The world seemed to tilt abruptly. Even clutching the hook she could not gain her balance. She felt herself pitching hopelessly backward into the void. In utter desperation she jerked her body back from the edge and slammed into the glass of the window. There was an instant's resistance, and then it shattered under her weight and sent her crashing headlong into the room.

It could not be Father. He was dead. Dead. And yet there he stood before her, looking exactly as he had the summer when she was fourteen. The grief and guilt she had carried for so long gave way to an impossible joy.

"I said, what are you doing there, Emily? It's long past

your bedtime." He was holding something in his hand—a jar of red paint and a brush.

She couldn't speak a word, couldn't move a muscle. The room she had been standing in moments before had vanished. She was now in the basement of the bungalow they had lived in that impossible summer. The furnace threw its branching limbs ceilingward like some metallic tree holding the house aloft in its arms. Beside her stood the cold room, its door slightly ajar, shadowed tins of food ranged on pale green shelves. On the lower shelf sat the broken clock she had torn her finger on while exploring its works one Saturday morning. Her baby finger still bore the scar. Behind her was the door to the basement room she had slept in back then. In the dimness she could see her bed, her desk, her diary lying open on it. If she ran upstairs now she knew she would find her mother sleeping on the pullout couch in the living room, Elizabeth and Charles lying in their beds in the small room beside. And at the back of the house, in the room that had once been hers, she would find Albert curled up at the bottom of his crib, his thumb tucked in his mouth. They would all be there; they had always been there, would always be there. She was overwhelmed by bliss. Tears welled up in her eyes.

All she could do was stare dumbfounded as her father began to move toward her, knowing in some faint far-off part of her brain that this was all an illusion of some sort, yet at the same time willing with all her heart to be seduced by the spell.

"What is it, Emily? Did you have a bad dream?"

"Yes, a bad dream," she said mechanically, watching him set the paint down on the edge of the table. His fingers were stained with it. A memory stirred. She looked at him and for an instant found herself staring at someone else entirely.

"I think perhaps you're still dreaming," he said, and his faced locked smoothly into focus. She followed his gaze as he looked down at the doll lying on the table.

The knife had left a deep cut above one eye. That eye stood open in a startled stare. The large nightgown hung limply well below its feet.

"We'd better not let your mother see this," he said. "It was hers, you know. I was fixing it for Albert."

"I'm sorry. I—"

"Yes, I know, dear. You were dreaming. You didn't know." He had come up behind her. His hands fell on her shoulders. They were cold.

"Oh, Emily. It hurts me to see you so troubled. Where's my bright-eyed little girl? Where has she gone?"

His words were like balm, sweet, soothing. She felt the dim terror of the dream drain away.

She looked down at the ravaged doll. How could she have done such a horrid thing? Why couldn't she remember? There had been something, some terrible urgency, something she knew she must do.

The doll fixed her with its wide eye. It caught her, held her. Its stiff puckered mouth seemed to stretch momentarily into a smile. The sweet plump face seemed lean and leering, the nightgown limp and bodiless on the bench. She stiffened at the sight.

"Is there something wrong, dear?"

His breath was hot upon her neck. As he reached down over her for the doll, she caught another, darker smell beneath the scent of roses.

On the table the doll stirred. Its stiff arms spread wide, its eyes popped open, and it stood.

Now, now. There's nothing to be afraid of. Nothing at all.

Father brought it up to her. She felt it nuzzle at her neck. It was cold, so terribly cold.

"I think it's time you went to sleep." He began to guide her toward her room. The arms of the doll closed tight against her throat.

No pain. Just a little sleep. No pain. Just . . .

"A little sleep and you'll feel much better."

A great yawning blackness opened under her. She felt herself spiraling slowly into it, panic fading quickly into peace.

"No, Mr. Dwyer! No!"

Alice stood on the bottom step, screaming.

The puppet loosened its grip on Emily's neck. She collapsed to the ground, gasping for air.

Mr. Dwyer stood there, the Devil dangling from his hand, staring at the girl on the stairs. For a moment he seemed to recognize her. He gave a light shake of his head, as if to clear it. The puppet fell with a crack to the floor.

"Mr. Dwyer, it's me—Alice."

But there was no recognition in those glazed eyes now, nothing. He began to move toward her, slowly, stiffly, like a windup toy. His face was powdered a deathly white; his lips stood out livid against them. She realized they had been painted red. He had made himself over into the image of the Devil puppet.

"I've come to take you under," he said as he advanced upon her. But the voice was not Mr. Dwyer's. It was the hoarse croaking of the Devil in the play. Terror whistled down her spine. Here was the creature from her nightmare, finally loosed from the pattern on the wall.

Over his shoulder she saw her aunt struggle to her feet

and turn toward the table. She reached for the knife that lay there, raised it above her head, then brought it down hard against the Devil's head. A splinter of wood flew into the air. Mr. Dwyer stopped dead. A look of utter confusion filled his face; she felt that for an instant again he recognized her; then the eyes glazed over and he turned.

Aunt Emily was hacking frantically now with the knife. Mr. Dwyer seemed to totter. His hands flew to his head. Emily raised her hands above her head and with one last mighty blow brought the blade down against the wooden skull. It split in two. For an instant a long inhuman shriek of fury filled the room, a shriek that seemed to keen from the shattered head, from Mr. Dwyer's slack mouth, from the dark depths of the basement itself. As it slowly died away Mr. Dwyer dropped in a crumpled heap to the floor.

Aunt Emily stood looking down at the shattered head of the puppet. The inside of the skull was spiked with thorns. The knife fell from her hand and clattered to the concrete floor.

Lela sat up shivering in her bed and looked around the room. Asha had fallen onto the floor. She scrambled out of bed, picked the doll up, and hugged her tight. Then, padding quietly across the room, she reached up and switched off the fan.

30

THE GARGOYLE HAD GONE TO SLEEP again in the stone. Its eyes were sealed, its features smooth and worn. Time had drawn its gauze of forgetfulness over it once more. In the shade of the cornice the scrollwork dragons curled about their crumbling hordes. They did not stir from sleep as, far below, a figure came through the gate and started up the flagstone walk.

Alice hurried up the stairs and through the door. The smell of furniture polish and old books greeted her; motes of dust floated lazily in the sunlight beneath the stained-glass dome.

The Ring for Service sign stood on the counter. From the end of the hall she heard the sound of glass being swept; a keen memory of nightmare knifed through the calm.

She found Mr. Dwyer in the workroom. He had shaved, trimmed his mustache, changed his clothes. Save for the dark circles about his eyes and the pallor of his skin, he looked again like the shy young man she had been drawn to months before.

"Good morning," he said.

"Good morning."

He dumped the dustpan full of splintered glass into the wastebasket. The garbage had been cleared from the counter, the dishes cleaned. A warm breeze blew through the broken window. Coffee bubbled in the percolator. The only note of unease was sounded by the hinged wooden box sitting in the center of the table. It might as well have been made of glass.

"We seem to have had a break-in," said Mr. Dwyer. "Although, to tell the truth, I'm not sure."

He motioned Alice to sit down. "You see, nothing seems to be missing." He stood with his back to her now, working shards of glass from the broken window.

In the distance she saw the rusted tower, the sunlit canopy of the woods.

"Alice, I'm afraid this is going to sound a little crazy. But I woke up yesterday morning on a cot in the basement, and I couldn't remember how I got there. I feel as though I've been living through a dream—a long, dreadful dream. None of it seems real."

He doesn't remember, she thought. He doesn't remember Saturday night—any of it.

"One of the puppets is ruined," he went on as he turned back to the table. "I found it on the basement floor." He opened the lid of the box. Couched on its limp cloth body lay the broken remains of the Devil. She looked down at it and felt nothing.

He reached in under the cloth and revealed the jewel-encrusted knife.

"This was lying beside it," he said. "Yes, it's the knife that was stolen from the display case. I wonder now whether I could have taken it myself, whether I was the one who did this.

"I have no idea how we're going to replace the puppet. The set is ruined. Yet somehow all I feel right now is relief, relief that it's all over."

Down the hall the bell on the desk sounded. He dashed off to see what it was. Alice was left alone in the room with the remains.

The skull had been split in two. That leering mouth was sundered now; those piercing eyes just two hollow pits in the ravaged wood. All that remained of its horror now were the barbed thorns that bristled like a chestnut burr from the inside of the shell.

Couched on the black cloth of its body were the blood red stones that had been its eyes. They were vacant now; gone was the gleam of malignancy that had smoldered in their depths. She picked one up, felt the heft of it in her palm, saw the dance of sunlight on its faceted surface.

As she glanced down at the knife lying on the table a sudden shock ran through her. On the side of the hilt there was a socket, circled with claws, where a jewel had once rested. Turning it over, she found another. With trembling hand, she took the red stone and lowered it to the knife. The claws took it smoothly in their grip; a vital piece of the mystery slid into place.

The next few days were a flurry of activity. First, a replacement for the Devil had to be found. They went through all the likely sets, hoping to unearth something satisfactory. There was a ghost figure from a Christmas play, which they experimented with but quickly realized would not work. In the end they decided there was nothing for it but to make a new puppet.

Mr. Dwyer had made puppets in the past and was familiar with the mechanics of it all. With Miss Witherspoon's book for support they set about shaping a clay form for the new head, which they then covered with several layers of paste-sodden newspaper strips. They would allow the paper to dry and then cut it away from the form, leaving them with a hollow head on which to work.

Most of the supplies they needed were to be found on the basement workbench, where Miss Witherspoon had made her own puppets. Of course, as was Miss Witherspoon's way, chaos reigned in her wake. The paints ranged on the back of the workbench were dried out and utterly useless and would have to be replaced. The brushes could not be found amid the clutter of boxes and cranny holes that rose against the wall at the rear of the bench. There were bits of cloth piled in abandon, among which they would no doubt be able to find something that would serve. But smaller items like scissors, needles, and spools of thread all had to be painstakingly ferreted out of hiding.

Mr. Dwyer had gone off to the craft store to buy the jars of paint they would need to complete the puppet head, as well as a new supply of brushes to do the job. He had left Alice alone in the basement to cut the head away from the clay form and apply the final layer of newsprint to the joined halves. It was a messy job. She had rolled up her sleeves and donned the old apron they had found balled up at the back of the bench. Underneath the rigid and regimented exterior Miss Witherspoon had presented to the world there had lurked a first-class slob.

Before Alice on the bench, Miss Witherspoon's book on puppetry lay open. While she worked, she glanced down at it from time to time, muttering snatches of dialogue to herself. They had decided, after all, to scrap Jacob Hubbard's ending in favor of the one in the book. Mr. Dwyer now agreed with her wholeheartedly that it was a much more satisfying conclusion to the play, and confessed that he had been wrong to cling so stubbornly to the original text. It meant more work for them both, but there was joy now in the work.

There had been some excitement at home the night before. After dinner, Mother had felt some mild contractions. Everyone went into a flurry, thinking she had gone into labor. Father got so excited that Aunt Emily made him go lie down. It turned out to be a false alarm. Still, it could not be long now.

Alice worked carefully, cutting the papier-mâché layer in two and working the halves carefully away from the clay mold. Above her, with creaks and groans, the old building settled into sleep. A latecomer rattled vainly at the front door, then dropped books through the slot into the night deposit box. Beyond the bright island of light around the workbench the basement was webbed with shadows. Yet those shadows held no terror for her now, only dusty boxes of books, bundles of magazines, retired equipment and furnishings, like the fond memories of an aging mind.

As she worked in the stiff old apron, sealing the halves of the puppet head together with paste-sodden strips of paper, she felt for all the world like Miss Witherspoon reincarnated, busily laboring at her love. Her hands moved with a sureness she had not felt before. The strips of paper went on effortlessly, with a skill she had no right to expect.

In no time she was finished. She wiped her hands on the apron, set the bowl of paste aside, and turned herself immediately to the task of finding a bit of material from which to cut the puppet's body. Her fingers sifted through the pile of scraps on the back of the table, pausing to consider one or another of them, but ultimately dismissing them all.

It was then that her eye fell upon a piece of black silk tucked into one of the cubbyholes in the wall behind the bench. It looked to be exactly what she needed. She reached over to pull it out. It would not come; a corner of it seemed to be caught on something. She gave a little tug—and stared in amazement as a rectangular piece of wood in the wall behind it came away.

A small compartment lay hidden behind it. She leaned forward, peered in, but saw nothing. She reached her hand in and felt around tentatively. Empty, of course. No—wait. Her hand, drifting farther into the hole, had fallen on something. It seemed to be a box of some sort, long and smooth, shaped something like a shoe box. And quite heavy, she discovered when she tried to lift it out.

Out in the light it proved to be a wooden box, hinged at one end and with a tarnished brass clasp at the other. She opened it and found that it was in fact a file box of sorts. There was a thick set of cards indexed and bound with a rubber band, and tucked in behind it a stack of correspondence tied with string.

One letter lay loose atop the pile, obviously a late addition. It was addressed to Miss Mabel Witherspoon. What was this, then? A secret trove of love letters that Miss Witherspoon had hidden away from the world? And what were these cards?

As she attempted to remove the bundle the elastic band snapped, and the cards spilled onto the table. They were of various ages, judging from their color, and all were covered with Miss Witherspoon's diminutive scrawl. Alice had to read no more than a couple of them to realize that what she had stumbled on here was nothing other than the missing catalog of the puppet collection. Each set was described in detail, including an itemized list of characters and properties, along with a note on the script, if any, that accompanied the set. In addition there were detailed notes on the history of the set and the manner in which it had been acquired for the collection.

This was the key to the whole of Miss Witherspoon's life's labor. But why had she hidden it away? Were there those around her whom she did not trust for one reason or another? Or was it simply her way of keeping it safe, so safe in fact that now it was only by the merest chance that it had turned up at all?

The letters in behind appeared to be correspondence relating to the acquisition of certain items in the collection: letters of inquiry about certain sets, of appreciation for items received—all quite boring. Alice more than half wished they had been love letters after all. The only one that held any mystery was the one still in its envelope, which had lain loose on top. She turned her attention to it.

The letter was from one William Dickson of Boston, Massachusetts, and concerned a certain puppet set formerly in his family's possession, which had been auctioned off among other items of the estate upon his father's death, and which he had reason to believe had recently come into Miss Witherspoon's possession.

The handwriting was of the same school as Miss Witherspoon's, verging on invisibility. It seemed to have been written in a fervor, for many of the letters were only half formed. It was a strain to read it, and had she not almost immediately come across something that piqued her curiosity, Alice would most certainly have set it aside.

The words that leaped out at her were "Punch and Judy." After a little puzzling it became apparent that the set under discussion was none other than the Punch-and-Judy set they were using for the performance. The name of Jacob Hubbard, the Punchman who had made the set and who was the author of the text of the play that accompanied it, was mentioned.

There were, it seemed, some things that Mr. Dickson wished to inform Miss Witherspoon of regarding the set, some disturbing events that had visited past possessors of it, of whom his late father was the last. He had sold the set in haste upon his father's death, happy just to be rid of it; but he found now that his conscience would not rest until he contacted the new owner.

"I am not a man much given to fancy," he wrote.

It is not in my nature. So I beg you to weigh what I have to say against that fact. The Punch-and-Judy set which is now in your possession belonged, as you no doubt are aware, to a certain Jacob Hubbard, a famous Punchman in these parts in the nineteenth century. His skill in the art was well documented in his day, and he was no stranger in the houses of the rich, where his show was commissioned to be performed on many festive occasions.

What is not so well known is that in addition to practicing the art of puppetry, this same Jacob Hubbard was rumored to be involved in arts of a decidedly darker nature. There were even those in his day who credited his uncanny skill in his craft to powers of a more than human kind.

In his early years, he often performed in company with a certain Professor Mephisto, a magician of sinister repute. People were generally of a more superstitious nature in those days, particularly the laboring poor, many of whom had brought their rural beliefs with them to the towns and cities where Jacob Hubbard plied his trade. Among the more enlightened segments of society such prejudices were rare; and as time went on and his fame grew, it was increasingly in those circles that Jacob Hubbard moved.

He became in time a wealthy man, but as is the case with many who experience sudden wealth, he was unsuited to it. He was given to excesses of various sorts, among them an inordinate fondness for drink. This—coupled with the fact that while other Punch shows changed with the times, introducing new figures and a generally more moderate tone, his remained stubbornly the same—ultimately proved his undoing. In the end he was shunned by those very benefactors who had at first embraced him.

His final years were eked out in poverty and dissipation. He took to the streets with the show again, but the age had passed Punch by. In the busy life of the city few found time to stop and watch and pay a penny to the Punchman. He went on the road and traveled through the smaller towns of New England, New York State, and on into Canada. It was on one such occasion that my great-grandfather saw the show.

Being of independent means, he had taken upon himself a chronicling of the lives of the street laborers and entertainers who were fast disappearing in his day. He befriended Jacob Hubbard and asked him home. He persuaded him to tell his history and to perform the show, which my great-grandfather duly transcribed word for word. This is the source of the text in your possession, which, according to Jacob Hubbard, was the same show he had performed for nearly thirty years.

My grandfather, then but a boy of five, was allowed to sit in the parlor while the Punchman performed the show and my great-grandfather wrote it down. In his later years, when the memory of childhood returned to him with unusual clarity, he would often speak of how terrified he had been, sitting there in the darkened parlor, watching the show. It was the figure of the Devil that most frightened him, and he had finally to be taken from the room so that his father could write.

This was in August of 1896. Shortly afterward, Jacob Hubbard died. A will was found on his person, willing the puppet set to my great-grandfather, and so it came into our family's possession. We had no real use for it and yet felt obliged to keep it. By and by it found its way into the attic, and it is there I still remember finding it shut away in an old trunk one summer when I was nine. I certainly didn't know what to make of it then. I had never seen such a thing as a Punch-and-Judy show. It was a mystery to me, yet for some reason it frightened me terribly, and after having opened it once I left it untouched thereafter.

It was not until the time of my grandfather's death five years later that I happened to see it again. As I have said, in his old age my grandfather thought continually of the time of his youth. It seemed more real to him than the world in which his old body now existed. He was given to wandering, and on more than one occasion a neighbor would call to say that he had wandered over to their place, was confused, and would we kindly come to pick him up.

On the last day of his life he had gone missing again. It grew dark and there was still no accounting for him. My parents were in a panic; none of the neighbors had seen him and a thorough search of our property failed to turn him up. There were medicines he had to take, medicines without which he would certainly die. My father was out all evening searching for him, driving up and down the country roads round about, hoping against hope to find him.

My mother and I waited up. But when midnight neared and he had still not returned, I was sent to bed. My room was on the upper floor. While walking down the passageway to my bedroom I happened to glance up the narrow flight of steps that led to the attic, and to my amazement I saw a dull light glowing beneath the door.

It was there I found him, lying on the floor by the open trunk, dead. The puppets were on the floor around him, along with the script of the show. On his hand was the Devil's head. According to the doctor, he had suffered a heart attack. That may be, for he was not a well man. But what I shall always be left with when I think of that August night is the look on his face when I found him lying there, a look of such unspeakable fear that even now it chills me as I write of it fifty-six years later.

The puppet set was put away for good, and I did not chance to see it again until my father's estate came into my hands on his death. I decided immediately to be rid of it. Along with several other items from the estate, it was put up for auction. The rest you know.

That is my story. Those are the facts. What those facts point to is quite another matter. I am, as I stated at the outset, not one normally given to fancy. But in this matter I must in the end side with those simpler souls of another age than our own, who first started the rumor that there was more than a merely human power in the art of Jacob Hubbard, that something of evil inspired that skill. That something, I feel, clings still to that puppet set, worked as it were into its very shaping, and waiting to be awakened again. I pray to God that it does not wake on you.

31

THE CHILDREN BEGAN TO GATHER around ten. Arriving piecemeal, in ones and twos, the younger ones accompanied by parents, they assembled in the Children's Room, browsing among the bookshelves while they waited for the show to begin.

Alice watched from the wings, going over the script one last time, absolutely convinced that once the lights went down and the show began she would instantly forget everything. Her stomach was knotted into a tight ball, her body limp with panic. She thought she might be sick.

She'd awakened early that morning. Thinking it would be far better to be up and around rather than lie in bed paralyzed by dread, she'd crept quietly downstairs. She had been sitting in the kitchen, watching the sun rise over the woods, trying to coax a bowl of cereal down, when Father came in for a coffee. Mother was having mild contractions, five minutes apart. He thought that he would stay home from work.

Mr. Dwyer had just opened the building when she arrived shortly before nine. Up until ten she had held out the bright hope that no one would show up, that for some reason or other the signs posted conspicuously around the building had all been blissfully overlooked. Even as the first few patrons wandered in she assured herself they were not there for the show at all, but had only happened by. She held out the hope for as long as she possibly could. By ten-fifteen, though, the room had begun to fill up; already the overzealous among them had begun to station themselves on the floor in front of the newly painted puppet stage. The unmistakable buzz of anticipation had overtaken the room; there was to be no reprieve.

She retreated to the bathroom. There, locked securely in the cubicle by the wall, she applied water-soaked wads of toilet paper to the back of her neck while she sat perched on the edge of the seat with her head hung between her legs. These maneuvers, half-remembered remedies for faintness she had read about somewhere, were designed to make her feel better. What they in fact made her feel like was the Victoria doll, doubled up in its carriage. She took deep breaths—also advised—and felt the water running down her neck.

This is ridiculous, her better self scolded her. There's absolutely nothing to be afraid of. Why, they won't even see you, for heaven's sake. You'll be hidden away behind the puppet stage. All you have to do is stick up your hand and say your lines.

Her better self could afford to be philosophical; it was not on the verge of throwing up.

The door opened. Voices entered.

"But I don't *have* to go to the bathroom."

"Nonsense. You go pee right now or we're going home."

"But I don't have to go."

"Listen to me, Catherine. You get on that toilet right now and go pee. I'm not going to get up in the middle of the puppet show to take you."

Two sets of feet appeared below the partition of the adjacent cubicle, one set large, in sandals and socks, the other small, in running shoes. A pair of pink shorts dropped down to join the running shoes. The mother came down on her haunches in front of her. Alice immediately sat up on the seat. One of the water-soaked wads dropped to the floor with a wet plop.

The mother, obviously aware now that they had company in the neighboring cubicle, noticeably changed the tone in her voice.

"Wait, dear, don't sit down yet. Let Mommy put toilet paper around the seat first."

"What's that?" Catherine had obviously noticed the wet wad.

"Shhh. Okay, sit down, dear. Now let's hear a little tinkle."

The tinkle took some time in coming. Alice suddenly realized that it must be almost time to begin. She flushed the toilet for show and hurried from the bathroom.

She was no sooner out the door than Lela and Aunt Emily walked into the library. She had not been expecting them, and the sight of them there brought on a new panic. Lela clung to Aunt Emily's hand. She carried Asha, resplendent in a newly knitted outfit, in her other hand. She wore an odd worried look as they walked up to Alice.

"I decided to come," said Aunt Emily. "Hope you don't mind. It won't make you nervous, will it, having us here?"

"No," Alice lied, "not at all."

Lela seemed very subdued indeed. She hardly took any notice of Alice at all, straining instead to see past her into the now noisy room. The lights had already been lowered; the painted theater appeared magical under the spotlight hung above the stage.

"Someone," said Aunt Emily with a downward nod at her charge, "was a little hesitant about coming, as you can no doubt see. I assured her it was all right now. I think it will be good for her to see for herself."

Alice caught sight of Mr. Dwyer over by the desk, motioning to her, pointing frantically at his watch. He was not exactly the picture of composure himself.

"I have to go," she said. "You'd better go in and find a seat."

"Yes." For a moment Alice sensed that there was something her aunt was about to say. It hung there awkwardly between them, unspoken; then she caught sight of Mr. Dwyer staring at them. A curious expression had stolen over his face. She quickly turned to go.

Aunt Emily called after her. "Oh, Alice?"

"Yes?"

"Good luck or break a leg or whatever it is one says."

"Thanks."

The chairs at the back of the room had all been taken, mostly by parents squeamish about sitting on the floor. At the fringes of the play area older children perched self-consciously on the edges of the tables that had been pushed away, dangling their feet. There was still a little space on the floor. Emily threaded her way with Lela through the thicket of small bodies until she found a space. She spread her sweater on the floor and sat down on it, settling Lela on her lap. Small faces turned to scrutinize the big one in their midst. She smiled and they turned away.

It was a very nice room, she thought. Full of air and space and a sense of history; not one of those pastel nightmares of steel and plastic that had ravaged many a library she'd been in. Her eye fell on the mural. How beautiful. How long, she wondered, before some fool would paint it over. Some things should be left as they were, and progress be damned.

Alice came into the room now, accompanied by Mr. Dwyer. They both wore black. As they walked to the front of the room a hush fell over the crowd. Emily wondered if she ought to have told Alice that, shortly after she'd left for the library, her mother had decided the pains were close and regular enough for her to go to the hospital.

No, it was best to wait until after the show to tell her. She had quite enough to think about now already, and there was nothing she could do, nothing any of them could do really, but hope all would go well. It would be a dangerous delivery.

The fetal monitor set off its steady beep as the baby's heartbeat danced across the screen. Mother lay back in the bed, her head propped up on pillows. A thin film of sweat beaded her upper lip. Father had stationed himself by her side. His hand rested lightly on her abdomen. He felt it begin to tighten now.

"Okay, love, here comes another one." Mother took a deep cleansing breath, readying herself for the onset of the contraction. They were coming in earnest now, two minutes apart. A succession of waves, rising, peaking, falling away. One was hardly over before the next began.

As the contraction built she breathed into the pain—light shallow breathing, rhythmic, controlled. She tried to ride the pain, to enter into it, rather than fighting it. She let her jaw go slack.

"Good, very good," encouraged Father. She clutched his hand, tightening her grip as the contraction gained in intensity. He looked at his watch. "Thirty seconds. Almost half over." He ran the damp cloth over her forehead. "Eyes open, love. That's the way. Just like that. Good, good."

She fixed her eyes on the photo taped to the rail of the bed—a picture of Lela that Father had brought along. Something to concentrate on through the pain.

"It's going now. It's almost gone."

She rode the wave slowly into shore, staring steadily into the wide eyes of her little girl.

Lela sat as rigidly in Emily's lap as Asha sat in hers. She studied the faces of the children seated around them, and watched the puppets onstage with a wary eye. But as the crowd broke into laughter at Punch's antics, she began by degrees to laugh with them, and Emily felt the tension slowly flow from her.

Could Lela hear her sister's voice behind the puppet, she wondered, or had the magic of imagination silenced all such thoughts? Magic. What was there more than magic in the end? These little lives of theirs, so precious, so desperately fragile—each one was an opening of magic.

How quickly one grew numb to the wonder of it, numb to the terror that was its twin. Time stepped in and spread its webs over the *Wonder Book*, covered in forgetfulness the wonder and the fear it held, which children felt so near.

Fear and wonder, joy and pain. How closely bound they were. Without the one the other could not be. It was a truth at times too hard to bear. One laid the wonder by to still the fear.

As she sat there in the darkened room, the fear she'd felt that night washed over her like a wave. She imagined the flier in its dusty case, the knife couched safely by its side, and for a moment the infinite weight of the building pressed down upon her, so that she could barely breathe.

But then the crowd laughed and Lela squirmed with delight on her lap, and as quickly as it had come it was gone.

Was it over then, forever? No, it could never truly be. The night would come around again, she knew. A darker magic dwelt among them here. The danger lay in forgetting, in refusing to see, in denying the dark side of the dream.

For now, though, it was done. She had been schooled for long enough in fear. She would study wonder now.

She glanced about the darkened room—the children cast in shadow, their eyes fixed upon the lighted stage; while other children, from the shadows of the woods above, looked to where the light broke through the leaves and a woman read a wonder book among the painted trees.

Alice peered out through the backdrop at the crowd before the stage. Her eye fell on Lela sitting on Aunt Emily's lap. For a moment it was as if she were looking at herself sitting on her mother's knee, while Miss Witherspoon worked her magic on the stage.

All her nervousness had gone. The lines had come alive. She had no need to consult the script taped to the wall beside her. She *was* Punch.

Mr. Dwyer worked busily by her side, his hand darting smoothly into the limp cloth figures ranged before him, bringing each one magically to life as it took its turn with Punch upon the stage. From time to time he turned to her and smiled. It was a smile that said they were doing well.

As the play went on Alice found herself feeding off the laughter of the crowd, feeling their sympathies for Punch fill her as well. The events of the past months played themselves out spontaneously in her mind, impossibly real. As they neared the climax of the show, she glanced out instinctively at Emily, for she could not help but feel as if the play were somehow celebrating their own victory. Yet Punch's triumph belonged not only to themselves, she knew; it belonged to all those out there watching in the dark as well.

PUNCH *lowers* KETCH *into the coffin and removes it from the stage. He returns with his stick, dancing about the stage, beating time with it.*

PUNCH:

> *Try as they will*
> *I beat them still,*
> *There's never a man to match me.*
> *And here's a stick to thump old Nick*
> *If ever he tries to catch me.*

Enter the DEVIL. *He peeps in from a corner of the stage, then disappears.*

PUNCH (*to audience*): What's that you say? There's someone there? Where? I don't see him.

Enter the DEVIL *from the opposite side of the stage. Peeps out, then disappears.*

PUNCH (*to audience*): What? Where? I don't see anyone. I'd thank you to stop fooling me.

Enter the DEVIL *from directly behind him. Taps* PUNCH *on the shoulder.* PUNCH *whirls around.*

PUNCH: Who are you?

DEVIL: I am the Devil.

PUNCH: The devil you are.

DEVIL: The devil I am.

PUNCH: And what the devil do you want?

DEVIL: I come for you, Mr. Punch. To carry you under.

PUNCH: No, no, please go away. I'm frightened.

DEVIL: No matter. You must come with me.

PUNCH: Oh dear! What will become of me?

The DEVIL *lowers his horns and runs at* PUNCH, *who evades him. He does it again, and again* PUNCH *darts out of the way, this time aiming a blow at the* DEVIL's *head. The* DEVIL *eludes it and many others that follow, rolling his head back and forth on the stage, while* PUNCH *brings the stick down on the boards.*

Exit the DEVIL.

The time for delivery was at hand. They wheeled the bed with Mother on it down the hall to the delivery room. Father donned a mask, a cap, and green coveralls and joined the doctor and nurses in the room. The doctor was stationed at the foot of the bed, seated on a stool.

"Okay, Elizabeth, I want you to push. Push hard."

"I can't. I have to keep breathing."

"No, not now, love," said Father. "Take a deep breath now, and push. Let that baby out."

Elizabeth took a breath, held it, pushed till her face turned red. Nothing. Again and again and again.

Finally, "There, I can see the top of the baby's head."

"Push again, Elizabeth. Push hard. We're almost there."

The DEVIL *reenters with a stick.* PUNCH *retreats to the side of the stage. They stand eyeing one another, make a few fencing passes. At last the* DEVIL *strikes a blow at* PUNCH *and hits him on the head.*

PUNCH: Oh, my head! What did you do that for? Please, Mr. Devil, let's be friends.

The DEVIL *hits him again.* PUNCH *begins to grow angry.*

PUNCH: Stop that! Stop it, I say; you're hurting me. Very well, if it's a fight you want, let's see who's stronger—Punch or the Devil.

A terrible battle takes place between the two. At first the DEVIL *has the upper hand, battering* PUNCH *at will with his stick. But he begins to grow weary and* PUNCH *lands several blows. The fight becomes equal for a time. Then* PUNCH *begins to get the better of the* DEVIL. *He drives him back across the stage, landing repeated blows on the* DEVIL's *head. The* DEVIL *falls to the stage, where* PUNCH *completes the victory, driving the breath from his body. He hoists the* DEVIL *high in the air on the end of his stick, whirling around and around.*

PUNCH: Hurrah! Hurrah! The Devil's dead.

"Okay, Elizabeth, push. One more time. There. There. Beautiful. Beautiful."

Cradling the baby's head in his hand, the doctor urged the tiny shoulder from the birth canal; it slid free and a fragile cry echoed through the room.

"Oh, look," cried Mother, tears running down her cheeks. "It's a baby. It's a baby."